Legends of the Slow Explosion:
Eleven Modern Lives

Legends of the Slow Explosion

ELEVEN MODERN LIVES

BARON WORMSER

TUPELO PRESSS *North Adams, Massachusetts*

Names: Wormser, Baron, author.
Title: Legends of the slow explosion : eleven modern lives / Baron Wormser.
Description: North Adams, Massachusetts : Tupelo Press, [2018] |
Series: Tupelo Press lineage series
Identifiers: LCCN 2018002044 | ISBN: 978-1-946482-10-5 (pbk. original : alk. paper)
Subjects: LCSH: Celebrities—History—20th century—Biography—Anecdotes.
Classification: LCC PS3573.O693 L44 2018 | DDC 811/.54—DC23

Cover and text designed and composed in Minion and Perpetua by Dede Cummings.

COVER ART: Yves Klein, "Le saut dans le vide, obsession de la levitation (Leap into the Void . . .)," (IMMA 21). October 1960: 5, rue Gentil-Bernard, Fontenay-aux-Roses. Artistic action by Yves Klein: copyright © Yves Klein estate, ADAGP, Paris / DACS, London, 2018. Photograph: Shunk-Kender copyright © J. Paul Getty Trust. Getty Research Institute, Los Angeles (2014.R.20). Additional permission granted by Artist Rights Society (ARS), New York; and by Art Resource, Inc., New York.

First paperback edition: April 2018.

Tupelo Press
P.O. Box 1767, North Adams, Massachusetts 01247
(413) 664–9611 / editor@tupelopress.org / www.tupelopress.org

Tupelo Press is an award-winning independent literary press that publishes fine fiction, nonfiction, and poetry in books that are a joy to hold as well as read. Tupelo Press is a registered 501(c)(3) nonprofit organization, and we rely on public support to carry out our mission of publishing extraordinary work that may be outside the realm of the large commercial publishers. Financial donations are welcome and are tax deductible.

ART WORKS.
arts.gov

Supported in part by an award from the National Endowment for the Arts

for Michael Steinberg and Richard Hoffman
and for Jim Schley

CONTENTS

PREFACE

SOME LIVES leave an imprint that is more than the sum of circumstances; such lives express the anima that is always floating around in the human ethos and that emerges in an imaginative action or series of them. It could be a woman refusing to give up her seat on a segregated bus or a painter indulging his passion for abstraction or a diplomat trying to parse out a very foreign society. The actions and the thoughts behind the actions form a skein that is identifiable in time but also has that haunting savor of the timeless, the realm of heroes and tricksters, paranoiacs and princesses. There is that feeling that some thread of spirit is being embodied.

The times this book treats of are modern times, specifically the second half of the twentieth century. It is the time of tremendous human invention, the true coming of mass society worldwide. It is the time when the word *new* becomes a value in its own ever-exciting right. It is the time that many writers in the first half of the century wondered about and feared: What will become of the human? Will truth be dismissed as an outmoded, inconvenient concept? Will the human race become robots or sleepwalkers?

Although the eleven lives I evoke in these pages tell different stories and although they come from wildly different backgrounds—Mr. Miles Davis, meet Mr. George F. Kennan—they speak from the era's Cold War heart. There is nothing remotely political about some of them—Anita O'Day, for instance—but for everyone the day-to-day course of life was lived under a huge nuclear shadow that has not gone away. The issue isn't so much how any one of these people was influenced by that shadow (though someone like Philip Berrigan was deeply influenced) as the annihilating strength of the shadow, the unnerving, headline feeling of everything giddily speeding up and everything ending. There is a desperate energy at work in modern times, the exaggeration bred by more and more machines. That energy swept people away even as it puzzled them. A Willem de Kooning had nothing to lose; a James Jesus Angleton had a great deal to lose. Either way, the compelling nature of the aggravated, exorbitant world they found themselves in could not be avoided.

I do not offer these legends as strict accounts. What interests me is the sense that something both larger and deeper than an individual life transpired. It is easy to lose that sense in the forests of detail, however important each of those details is. I respect those details and have evoked many of them in these pages, but at some point we have to ask the larger question: What was that about? If we cannot trust the bold outlines an exceptional life creates, then we have little to go on as we move blankly forward in the modern times of another century. To query a series of lives lived within the same era is to ask what stature was present and what wisdom a life could obtain. We seek to cloak ourselves in reason but exaltation and strangeness, insult and desire all beggar that reason. When George Harrison first heard Elvis Presley's voice or when Hannah Arendt, the arch European, began to see the United States for herself, something happened that emanated from the myriad linkages of time and place, and that had not happened before. From the hectic and often overbearing aura, a shaft of recognition emerged.

Legends of the Slow Explosion: Eleven Modern Lives

But, as far as legends are concerned, we can describe them, and, for a moment at least, believe that we have dispelled them.

from "The Enigma" by Albert Camus (1950)

—

History died; he gathered in its forces;
The mists of time condensed ...

from "Merlin Enthralled" by Richard Wilbur (1953)

ROSA PARKS

WHERE IT STARTED WAS UNCERTAIN. There was Africa. There were the ships. There was the auction block: twelve bucks for sale, ages twelve to twenty, and two wenches. There were thousands of wombs available to the master and his sons. There was the dinner table, "Pass the bread. Pass the butter. Pass the Negroes who are as much our property as the bread and butter. Pass the complaints about how shiftless they are. Pass the complacency that enables us to sit here and not think twice. Pass Senators Sparkman and Hill and their stentorian predecessors. Pass the iced water. Pass the states' rights. Pass this damned heat so it leaves the room. Pass the Bible that sanctions slavery. Pass those biscuits that Aunt Mary made. She makes the best biscuits. Pass the filibuster. Pass the birthright that is fate, born mewling and shrieking. Pass the whip. Pass the River Jordan. Pass the occasional kindness. Pass the way of life. Pass the mistress of the house staring into a disconsolate mirror."

Behind the path to the cabins, behind the preacher's sermon, behind the voices raised to heaven, behind the woman struggling with Humiliation, Indignity, and Viciousness, a Montgomery Alabama public transit bus heaved into sight with its human freight—white and black, coming home from work. They sat in their designated areas: whites up front, blacks in the middle until more whites appeared when they had to move to the rear of the bus which was the black area. If whites needed a seat, the driver would tell a black person to move. That was the law. The driver was an officer of the law and carried a gun. Everyone had to respect the law. If people did not respect the law, the world, as Montgomery knew it, would end.

There is that weight of how-things-are here. Everyone is born into that weight and that weight becomes part of who a person is. The weight can be favorable on account of your skin color or not favorable. The weight is larger than just one person, so any one voice is more than one person speaking. Everything concerns the weight, especially when the weight becomes a code. There were water fountains for white and colored but the colored fountain did not have colored water. "Colored" meant people. It wasn't, however, just the physical indignities, to say nothing of cruelties, but the mental ones that made the weight so vast. The weight was like one big mind that went everywhere every moment and never slept. The weight was a power that could strike at any time. You could be minding your own business but you had no "own business." The weight owned your thoughts—or at least tried to.

A child was bound to ask about why she couldn't go up to a certain fountain but had to use another one. A child was bound to say that it made no sense. And the adult was bound to look at the child and wonder how to explain. The adult was bound to wonder why she or he brought the child into a world filled with such soul-killing prohibitions. Perhaps the adult gripped the child's hand a bit more tightly and said, "That's the way it is." Perhaps the child heard in the voice a regret that no smile could absolve. Perhaps that tight grip almost hurt.

Everyone knew Rosa Parks was a serious, dignified, Christian woman: a serious, dignified, Christian woman who wasn't fit to take her own seat on a bus and stay there regardless of whoever else got on the bus. But "everyone" meant black folks not those white folks to whom Rosa Parks was just another Negro, to say nothing of the common epithet. She wasn't a real person but the coordinates of a few centuries of bad history. Everyone had learned to live with that bad history—that was what the bus was about. Some people actually celebrated the history. They had their pride and let everyone know it. If only they had won that war. Others, the unreal Negroes, simply had to live with it and take what they could, which was plenty in the way that being on the earth and sharing the earth with other people could be plenty. No pity need apply. But even the greatest vitality and love would have to move for the bus driver.

A person, black or white, could wonder about what sort of God blessed the circumstances of history. A person could wonder what God saw, if He saw anything. A person could wonder whether God was blind—loving and kind, no doubt, but blind. When the bus boycott began in Montgomery, after Rosa's refusal to move and her arrest, very few white folks, most of whom, presumably, were churchgoers, stood up for the Negroes. There were some, like the woman who directed the library and who was vilified for her support and killed herself not long after. If you stepped out of line, you could pay a pariah's price.

According to all manner of doctrine, people had free will despite the constraints people put on other people. Above that less-than-edifying spectacle, God resided in His appointed heaven and Rosa had faith in that God, if not explicitly in that heaven. You needed the buttress of spirit to stand up to what was determined to belittle you. The Negro ministers called upon the buttress of God day and night, their exhortations filled and enlivened the mute air, but the librarian lady fell down. She was in a congregation of what may have seemed like one. The God of the white churches offered consolations that apparently were not for everyone.

The librarian's demise might have been called a tragedy but that word did not apply to history, that word came from some other, ancient world, not an American one. Any little human life was just that—a little human leaf on the very big current of history, to say nothing of destiny. No one could see a leaf going down the Mississippi. You could see a person go under or you heard about it but plenty of people went under. Routinely, Negroes were murdered and nothing was done about it. The lives of Negroes were more like weeds in the eyes of those who controlled history. You could pull a weed and throw it aside and that was the end of it. Rosa easily could have gone under, too. Rosa easily could have been tossed aside.

A diet of loathing makes for some thin people. There was much pep and cheering from the white folks, waving pennants at the Sugar Bowl and the Cotton Bowl, finding religion in football, acting like grown-up children. Imagine! All the real trouble in the world and there they were: people getting worked up about a game. The shouting, though, the amplitude they prided themselves on, never made the white folks any larger. They stayed thin, their spirits starved, living on a ghostly animus, their self-respect tied, overtly or covertly, to denying the right to the same schools and books, their every motion and word a contrivance to which they held onto for unhappy, if accustomed, life. Everything was feeding white folks—their banks and their land and their colleges and their companies—but they remained lean and ever hungry. Out there in the dark nights of their heads lurked the Negroes with their demands and their very being that spoke of suffering that never should have been allowed. It didn't matter how great the Virginian presidents were or how great the generals were in the War Between the States. Some things weren't about greatness. They were about decency.

The Negroes lived, of course, in unnoticeable circumstances and a Negro woman was particularly unnoticeable. Then again, even if they had noticed, no white person would have asked Rosa Parks what she thought or how she felt as she went about her life as a seamstress in Montgomery. Those would have been senseless questions. To move to the back of the bus was still to be chattel—you Negroes back there. It was to be faceless and nameless, lost in the slave hold of anonymity. So to insist that you had a voice that could say something more than "Yes, sir" was as crucial an assertion as a Negro (and a woman, to boot) could make. Acquiescence and silence went together. The beauty of uprooting that acquiescence was that all those Bible-laced speeches that emanated from the Negro churches in Montgomery, a torrent of eloquence as noteworthy as any unleashed by the orators and ministers of the nineteenth century, stemmed from a brief non-discussion on what purported to be a public bus. Mrs. Parks was not moving. There you had it.

Ever since she was a child, Rosa Parks took herself seriously, the way any child raised by any responsible parent should be.

One of her strengths lay in her refusing to let go of that seriousness. Inequality neither bemused nor frightened her. It was more
like a taunt that never stopped ringing in her head and that was
personal. Her life was singled out for the arcane and obvious practices of subordination along with countless others. Her life could
be discounted. What had the United States Constitution said?
Three-fifths of a person.

Negroes had forever refused to be such fractions. Before and after World War Two, some of the discounted had protested. Some of
them in Alabama, the heart of Dixie, had gotten in touch with the
nefarious NAACP. Some of them had recognized the ultra-nefar-
ious Communist Party as being a very rare group that was willing
to take on murderous racism. What was the Cold War to someone
who couldn't drink at a water fountain? What were all the foreign
policy shenanigans and talk of the free world to someone who had
to move to the back of the bus?

How rarely, though, did a hypocrite see him- or herself in the
mirror. Maybe never.

Red Tool! Commie Plant! Un-American! The headlines shrilled
and in the way that headlines worked, a worthless accusation was as
good as a fact. Some of the people trying to help southern Negroes
in the 1940s, and whom Rosa had met, were connected to the Party.
Such ties made her not someone advocating the overthrow of the
government but someone who wanted to vote for a government.
Voting was something that older Negroes could only shake their
heads about. The right had been there once but it had gone. There
were tests and rules and for good measure a tax.

It was hard for them to imagine that right coming back as a
right, not something a person had to beg for, but Rosa could imagine it quite well. She was one of those people who were not afraid to

be stubbornly patient, full of a quiet inner fire, who would knock on the insensate door again and again until someone answered. "What do you want?" the voice might say. More likely, "Get lost." Or the voice would only grunt, not even bothering with a "No." What was there to talk about? Still, she knocked, as when she traveled around Alabama in the 1940s gathering information that she sent on to the national NAACP office about cases of violence against Negroes, murders and rapes that went unpunished, or frame-ups that could result in a Negro's death penalty. All it took was a white woman's accusation about a Negro man and hell could happen very quickly. The State of Alabama had its integrity to uphold.

"Schooled in contempt," she might have said, she who did not get the real schooling she hungered for, but there was no time to waste on grudges. She had seen how the impossibility of being in two places—black in a white world—led more than one person to a violent death, someone who could not take it anymore and struck back. There was no hope in striking back but the impulse made sense. There was also good sense in having a gun in your house and being ready to use it. Everyone understood a gun. In a nation where the federal government could not even pass an anti-lynching law, where opposition to such a law was, according to one southern senator, "a cause worth dying for," a gun spoke many rough volumes. Ask the Klan. Ask the anonymous callers who called up her house and made promises about her death.

How to get from here to there? How to get from the back to the front? How to get from talking to doing? How to get from typing endless letters and reports about endless wrongs endured by the powerless to achieving some measure of power? How to get from the nothingness that was impressed upon a person like some terrible duty to the somethingness that was a person? How to get from deference to assertion? How to get from a personal faith in God to a faith shared among sinners and for sinners, a faith that brought people together all the time not just one day a week?

A woman like Rosa Parks could believe in herself but to believe in others—that was a task. Centuries stood up and smiled a belligerent grin, which said, "You can't do it together. You're too weak. You're cowards. You believe what we've told you to believe." There was plenty of painful truth in that grin. And if as a Negro you gained a tenuous grip on something like prosperity, practicing some profession or owning a business, then why should you endanger what you have worked so hard to get? Status was easy to throw away for those who did not have it. For more or less middle-class black folks who had something, there was no need to agitate. They had figured out the rules well enough. They knew that nasty, shit-eating, what-are-you-going-to-do-about-it grin—how could they not?—but they managed their ways around it. That managing was nothing to sneer at, yet was pitiful in its way. Their reward wasn't so much half-a-loaf as a heel no white person wanted.

To believe in what white folks claimed was justice opened a person up to being called, at best, an idealist, and at worst naïve or even an outright fool. Did Rosa really believe they, who had all the power, would give in? Wasn't the scenario of rights being claimed and granted just something that made her go, that kept her earnest head busy but had no connection with reality as it had been practiced in Montgomery for what felt like time immemorial? Maybe it was true about her being an idealist, a believer in what she was owed, if not in the people who owed it to her. The deeper point was whether all the meetings, workshops, letters, and attempts to register added up to something like momentum or were bound to dissipate like water in a sieve. You see your life run out so there's nothing in that sieve: it hurts bad.

Inside Rosa the momentum kept growing. Whether she kept a diary or not, the moments were keeping track of her, the indignities did not let go. She had seen plenty of Negroes who lost their dignity. She didn't scold them or speak ill of them. She knew she would not let it happen to her—except that it felt bound to happen if she stayed where she was. Many days she avoided the bus because of the indignity, but not every day. So when the moment came of being asked to move and she refused, it was like time finally splitting open. Every last moment was there: the child walking to school, the adolescent learning how little the white world cared for her, the adult who was steadfast in her goals. No angels chorused. No band played. There was only an aggrieved bus driver and various furtive eyes on other seats. What is this? It was a question that deserved to be asked aloud each segregated day but wasn't.

So when she sat there waiting for whatever was going to happen next, maybe to be arrested, maybe hit or shoved or thrown off the seat or spat on or at least be called a "black bitch" because anything could happen, there was no need for explanation. The deed had been done. This determined woman was it. There was no getting past her. She had blocked the accustomed course of obedience. She might as well have been a mountain there on that bus. All her spirit congregated in her unmoving body.

Rosa Parks believed in a higher power but she also believed in her own power. God did not create people to make them negligible creatures—any of them. That belief gave her confidence. A person had stature. She claimed that stature ever since she was a girl and she had no intention of relinquishing it. If white people thought they knew more, that was their laughable conceit. There was no arguing with conceit. It acted how it acted—putting on its pathetic, superior airs—but there was no need to pay it any serious mind. The higher power meant exactly that. White people liked to act as if they were the final court and judgment but they weren't. A few of the honest ones might have admitted as much but most of them were glad to pretend as if they wrote the Bible. They wrote a bible of race but that was a very different story.

Tell me how it happened: a command that was voiced over and over, children asking parents and grandparents over generations— how tricks were played and how subtle insubordination played out and how white folks, however much they had the upper hand, were continually misled. Rosa Parks, a most upright woman, became part of that long-standing fabric of subversion. There seemed, at first or any glance, to be no place for such truth-tellers in the annals of resistance, nor did there seem to be any place for women who refused to do as they were told, much less women who prided themselves on that refusal. But there was a place. When Rosa stayed in her seat, it was the same as someone jumping over the moon and the sun in one defiant bound.

HANNAH ARENDT

SHE HAS WITNESSED RANT that silenced every reproof. She has waited for some larger affirmation to arise, the vision of decency, but none came. She has heard the triumph of jack-booted certainty strutting to the mob's approving roar. The precious freedom that a republic cherishes, the freedom to seek truth in the face of falsehood, can dissolve like a book left out in the rain. Heinrich, her edgy, shrewd, passionate husband who fought on the streets of Berlin is that precious, more precious, but without this freedom he would not be alive nor would she: two more corpses in the ideological charnel house of Europe. She does not doubt the burden: people must be ready to die for freedom, but the reasons must be honest ones. All the standard human debilities—greed, prejudice, sloth, ignorance, hypocrisy—are woven into freedom's cloth. Working as she does in the service of reason, she spends her life disentangling those threads, which is, in the twentieth century, a colossal joke. Some days she broods; some days she forgets. She is only human herself. At odd moments, Heinrich gently reminds her of that datum. He points out a tic in her German or a run in her stocking. They laugh together. There is something remarkable about their laughter. It is resonant with the distress and joy of time, moments that include kisses and years shattered by the hyphenated demiurge the two of them call "World-History."

History is the unexpected that is then parsed out as the expected. "Ah, yes, the world wars, Hitler, Stalin, revolutions, the atomic bomb; ah, yes, we saw it all coming. Here are some explanations." The human capacity for arguing backwards is as bottomless and frightening as the human capacity for accepting whatever comes marching down the disastrous pike. She and Heinrich are not mass people. The entertainments that light up Times Square could disappear tomorrow and for them there would be no loss. It isn't that they don't have fun—a word Americans are fond of. They are lots of fun—drinking, talking, and giving parties where people occasionally make tipsy fools of themselves. Their New Year's Eve parties are famous. But someone like Plato is likely to show up in their talk, a candle from the dim vault of profound endeavor. Would it be fair to say that Hannah is more at home with the philosophers than with the people down the hall? Sometimes she worries about that. She is an instinctively warm person. So many philosophers were cold men intent only upon the vigorous elaborations of their unhappy brains. They constructed intricate systems to catch flies.

She is safe in America—and thankful for that safety—but she is always looking over her shoulder. She turns around on a street off Broadway and sees only another New Yorker in his or her coffin of an overcoat. The sight reassures her. She goes forward on her errand, but for her larger errands there are no reassurances—nor should there be. Everything is fraught.

The person in the overcoat walks on unperturbed by the fraughtness. What would the German noun for that be? English is a terse, physical language incapable of those long words that gobble up short words. The German language was made for philosophizing. German honored the invention of entities. English was made for ordering fish.

She turns around again to watch the person. She has dwelled inside of life's fraughtness—love affairs, emigration, fanciful yet demanding conversations into the early hours of the morning—but she is outside, too. How could she ever have imagined she would be living here in New York City? Her childhood in Königsberg seems immeasurably far away. There were still landaus and teams of great, shaggy horses to pull them. There were rose gardens. There was the silence of a world before the advent of so many machines. German history, though, can clear any nostalgic vapors.

Juden raus!

How could a nation go so wrong? The first answer might be that it never was right. It wouldn't be a bad answer. Heinrich has proposed it to her more than once. Germany was never benign. As a nation, it had from the beginning too many dire myths rumbling in its stomach. The Jews always lived on a window ledge there. Good citizens, they partook eagerly of whatever crumbs were offered them; they made themselves comfortable on that ledge. They dressed properly, spoke properly, and educated their children properly. They loved German culture with an almost indecent passion. Hannah could quote Goethe and Heine with the best of them. If Jewish life was historically built on wariness then the belief in assimilation was all the more understandable. The Jews wanted to be part of the world that was Germany. Hannah *was* part of that world.

In her apartment are books and tobacco. Cigarettes give each day a harsh yet agreeable edge. A flourish of sorts, they intensify both the *longueurs* and flashes that go with thinking and conversing. One draws in and then expels. One reads and writes. Periodically she airs out the apartment but the city is dirty with the exhaust of smoke stacks and autos. That is as it should be. People are here to make money. The United States, as she once informed her mentor Karl Jaspers, is "a society of job holders." That is a fragile cohesion; everyone busy at whatever task they deem worthy of their precious hours. But maybe it is no more fragile than any cohesion. It emanates from the people. No king or church decreed this endless American labor. It makes for a bustling solace. Everyone has something to do. There are not so many grievances here. Yet she sees Negroes every day. There are plenty of grievances.

She has never been one for teleology. Ends tend to be lies that placate the means. Ends dwarf any mere life. What remains appalling to her about Germany was the eagerness of people to give themselves up to the ends and their indifference to the means. What happened there had nothing to do with the patient work of thinking but with faith gone wrong. Faith should be humble. Faith that is vengeful is a nightmare. So the ghastly assertion: Germany is a great country that must avenge itself, and part of Germany's greatness is its willingness to stand up against the forces that compromise its greatness. Murdering children—what a sign of greatness! Sometimes Hannah finds herself shaking her head on the street then she realizes other people shake their heads, too. They, too, have their inner conversations. They, too, carry within them the splinters of the past.

There is in this world no shortage of matters to despise. She can be a despiser. People who turn away from making judgments are at best too comfortable, at worst cowards. She has seen people be tested by history and fail. Many were friends of hers, people who, it seemed, shared her values and beliefs. One was once her lover. How hard for her to get that straight, to understand how a person of such depth could be susceptible to nothing more complex than the afflatus of hatred. Heidegger thought he was going to stand on a world stage. Trumpets would sound all around him. Spirits would levitate. The impulses that over two thousand years ago fashioned the tense embrace between the mystical and the rational would reappear with him as their emissary: a dream to mock all dreams. Yet something remarkable stirred inside of him. Though she was not much more than a girl when she went to bed with him, she knew that. Taking him into her body was like taking something imperishable into herself, something beyond flesh. If there was plenty there to shake her head about, there was nothing to regret. She had welcomed him. She had been flattered. And she had yearned for him. He trafficked in the impossible. He wasn't a modern man. When history knocked on his door, he thought it was his own legend summoning him. Alas, it wasn't. But *alas* was far too weak a word.

Juden raus!

Aspiration makes for a dangerous compound. That seems one of the beauties of living in the United States. There are no essences to aspire to. Beyond what a ballplayer can do, no one cares about greatness. The shop windows hold what is within reach. Money, in its fairy tale potency, beckons and inveigles.

She, too, enjoys lingering to look at a pair of shoes or a dress. The call to something higher has little appeal when considering a hemline or fabric. The vanity, whether mild or deep, that underlies every look in the mirror abets the commercial republic. That, too, is as it should be. People cannot escape their bodies nor should they want to. What destroyed Germany was the frightening mix of medieval and modern, obedience and degradation, kings and factories, everything wanting to be over and above and beyond, a *Götterdämmerung* of unsanctified emotion. Here, beyond the endless slogans, there are no sirens. The storefront medley of prices, bargains, and sales that accompanies her route along upper Broadway to the butcher, the grocery, and the five-and-dime is tawdry but blessedly mundane. Though no advertising agency is going to seek her out to pose for a photograph, she can appreciate the goods America dispenses: she is at home with her refrigerator as much as the next hausfrau.

How wrong that opponent of the mundane Karl Marx was! To think of him in the context of her daily life is almost humorous. A vengeful man, he could not accept the tangible rewards of capitalism nor could he believe that work might be more than a victim's begrudged labor. He lacked the combination of yearning, desperation, and common imagination that drove so many to America's shores. Instead, he sat in England and drove his pen to prove his loathing of the bourgeoisie. What he possessed, like many a Victorian, was a taste for fairy tales, only his fantasies ran elsewhere: the state would wither; labor would be replaced by higher activities; the working class would triumph.

The depredations of her adopted country are what they are. They have been practiced on the Negroes as something like a folkway, at once vicious and matter-of-fact. But there are laws and they can be brought to bear. There is a constitution. Marx, despite the shelter Britain afforded him, did not have a respect-for-the-rule-of-law bone in his prophetic body. He saw the careful precedents of justice as one more fraud. Those precedents can and do fail, as they have failed the Negroes, but democracy allows people to persevere. Such perseverance annoyed Marx. People with their quirks and peccadilloes annoyed him. A believer in the genius of theory and systems, he was one more progenitor of the false sciences that captivated the nineteenth century and set fire to much of the twentieth. He provided the justification for absolving any semblance of conscience: the masses—to say nothing of those who led the masses—have the right to bury the individual. *Bury* was not an exaggeration.

How many European intellectuals still worshipped at his sooty altar? Her husband once did. How many replaced God with history and a handful of exhortations? How many of them secretly believed that Soviet man and woman were better creatures? And how many despised America because it was irredeemably mediocre—the home of chewing gum and hair tonic?

Understanding the new nation has taken time. She would have been glad to live in France or, of course, Germany, but World-History ordained otherwise. America is such an unsettling mix of social friendliness and political covertness, of the prosaic and the idealistic, of oppression and freedom, of modern times grafted onto the world of 1776. For someone who has spent her life beginning many a sentence with "Why," America is bound to shock. That is the last question anyone cares for here. What matters is what you do, not what you think. It is hard for her to imagine a nation not as the complex sum of centuries but instead as an enterprise where everyone strives to achieve happiness. Happiness! Despite the brisk handshakes Americans exchange and the psychological explanations they lap up, happiness is no business. To found a nation based on the pursuit of happiness was to invite the personal into the political in ways no one could imagine. Hannah, who relishes etymologies, is quick to point out that *hap* means chance, luck, fortuity.

From chance to tragedy is a half-step, as when her friend Walter Benjamin committed suicide because on the particular day in 1940 he tried to enter Spain, he was turned back. It is the trail of steps that led her sister to commit suicide. Clara had sought love she never found and wept often about her unhappy fate. Was it her fault the men she pined for did not respond? To talk of happiness can be very cheap talk.

Perhaps the lack of consolation is what the consolation of philosophy can best teach. Abstraction is a dubious consolation, more gauzy absence than actual presence. Jaspers likes the word "concrete" to describe what philosophy must be. The real rigor of philosophy is to keep the world in front of you and not elevate or subjugate it. The real consolation is the integrity that may reside in thinking and the choice of not surrendering to the hypothetical. In that sense she feels at home in America. The clamor about what irrefutably exists is genuine. If it is short-sighted, a species of perpetual-motion machine, it is preferable to some murderous, sovereign goal. "Everyone here is busy. Everyone here muddles along." That would be another conundrum to chew on as she walks the short blocks of Broadway.

Some days there is literally music in the air, not the classical music that her sister Clara practiced on the piano and that Hannah was taught to adore, but popular American music. Stores on Broadway sell radios, record players, and records. She has found herself standing outside a store on a warm day and taking in the sound. "Noise," poor Clara, who played the piano beautifully, would have called it: no rapture, no grandeur, no impassioned sensitivity. To Hannah, who to her mother's chagrin had no special musical aptitude, the songs, however thin they first appear, are wonderful. They lack the cabaret edge of Weimar but are blessedly free of indulgent German sentimentality.

Someone named Dinah Washington is singing "September in the Rain." Hannah stands there—it is July—and listens. The woman's voice is full and sweet, precise and gracious and, in its crisp yet feeling way, exquisite. What more, Hannah thinks, could we ask of life? A Negro woman stops beside her and also listens. Here is a spontaneous plurality.

Too often, politics, with its necessary focus on the plural that is the people, is wrong-headed. "Society," Tom Paine wrote and she has quoted, "is produced by our wants, and government by our wickedness." Our wants are like the songs: love me and understand me. But our living with one another, our plurality, is something else. Conceit and distrust bleed into our mutuality. Degradations become accepted manners; cultivated loathing overturns whatever modest civility a society may have achieved.

Maybe until you have lived fearing a knock on the door that will mean your death, until you have experienced how the arbitrary and wanton can be a law unto itself, you cannot understand the importance of civility. The United States of America is the result of a revolution—an uncivil act—but one the world has yet to understand, an obscured and partial revolution tied to the rights of the individual. How are such individuals from all over the globe supposed to make a political society devoted to something other than glorifying selfishness? Does one right get in the way of another right? Do individuals start to see themselves as compendia of rights? Do they invent new rights? How are the rights shared if they are rooted in the individual's actions and sense of life? Must the exigent force of economics make a travesty of rights? In trying to answer those questions she is trying to assess the nature of that revolution. The revolution in America rarely impressed her leftist, European friends. A tolerant, wary, eighteenth-century view of humankind seemed beside the point in modern times. Yet here was this nation.

If human nature is unknowable, like the German saying about jumping over your shadow, then every political system is a less-than-educated guess. The challenge is to balance your guesses based on what you know about human beings—their wants and their wickedness. One of the errors of modern times was to disbelieve in wickedness. On the shelf of idiot bromides, progress stood out as one of the most stupid. Hegel—to choose one of her German forebears—was barking at eternity: history had no immanent direction. As a man entranced by teleology, he lacked a sense of his own conceit.

She has seen the wickedness at first hand. *Juden raus!* Those two words are the gist of many lifetimes; grief and calamity linking hands over centuries. Though she never goes to a synagogue, she is adamant about being a Jew. Like many a modern person, she knows that she has replaced God with the world. She can't help herself. The thread that connected her to the divine was snipped. The political news she retails to Jaspers in her letters about Joe McCarthy or Adlai Stevenson or the dubious character of Lyndon Baines Johnson is not the stuff of piety. Too often, it is the stuff of low-minded democracy, of rumor, calumny, and supposition.

Does this mere spinning world give a person sufficient light in which to view wickedness? There are examples and reasons—some better, some worse—but the light is something different. She and Heinrich talk about that light. She, after all, wrote her doctoral thesis about Augustine. To dissolve human wrongdoing in the great encompassing light of God is terribly easy. God diminishes mankind. Mankind exalts God. God exalts mankind. Mankind diminishes God. Such a topsy-turvy relationship is awful and comfortable at the same time like a child who will not stop shaking a rattle.

She has her particular fears, not only the mortal ones such as that Heinrich will die before she does, but ones that have no dimensions. Those are the modern fears bred in the bones of *banality*, a word Jaspers used in a letter to her after the war. The word is an answer of sorts to the obedient wickedness of functionaries but not an answer, more like a gambit. The problem of evil, as she has termed it, is, however, no chess game.

How can a condition be a problem? How can myriad acts contain one seed? How can reason apprehend the depredations of spirit or worse, the blankness of spirit, the vicious emptiness of the Nazi bureaucrat Eichmann doing his job and complaining about his rivalries with other functionaries? And doesn't "problem" insinuate an answer? Doesn't "problem" contain a mocking overtone: Hannah hefting her small, resolute shovel before a mountain of confusion? Banal or not, evil is bred in human bones. Other animals cannot do it. So all the categorical human issues—will, volition, choice, responsibility, morality—congregate outside a philosopher's door and beg to be heard. Philosophy, as Heinrich's beloved Socrates demonstrated, is an unlucky and largely unwanted practice. To do it is to suffer it.

Hannah suffers gladly. She has that outsider gene. She is the one who will always ask the uncomfortable question, the one who falls, as she says, between the stools. There is some pride in her about this. There is some contempt for those who refuse to follow the trail of questions through the tenebrous woods. There is ardor, too, though, and something like love. Because she loves to be in the world, she feels she owes the world her complicated honesty. Whether the world wants such honesty is, as she would be the first to testify, another story.

Perhaps what ailed Germany has ailed her, which is one reason she went to Adolf Eichmann's trial. Amid the famous German efficiencies—getting trains to concentration camps on time—there is the metaphysical impulse, the belief that thinking can be more than window dressing for prejudice. Questions and problems beg for solutions: Hitler, though not a metaphysician, had a final one. Of course, to impugn philosophy in that regard would be unfair. Philosophy is provisional, part of a Western tradition of thought-work that has striven to be impartial, though not objective. Judgments are crucial to living on earth. Without the judgments bred by conscience human beings are lost. To be objective in matters of heart-feeling is to surrender one's birthright. It grieves her that so many have been so eager to do so. *Inhumanity* is not an idle word. It means something very exact.

Juden raus!

Eichmann seemed in that glass booth a small, middling person, in his earnest way ridiculous. His certified Jew-hatred—how else had he managed to occupy such an important position?—took a back seat. Time and again over the months of his trial, he spoke not to his zealousness but to his honor and his deportment. He scraped before his betters and looked down on ruffians. He admired Hitler for making something of himself. While extermination was being organized on a scale hitherto unimaginable, he worried and chafed about his career. He confessed himself happy at some times during the war and frustrated at others. He took satisfaction in doing a good job, in being an expert of sorts about Zionism. He relished the tepid oblivion of cliché. This Nazi, he declared, was "brilliant," that one was "untrustworthy." As a bureaucrat, officialese gave him great pleasure.

The deaths—to descend into the world of words—were ghastly but the fact of this man insisting on his career was also ghastly. Hannah Arendt's tone in her reporting on the Eichmann trial was tinged with exasperation and sometimes with sarcasm. Who could fathom the disproportion between men sitting at their desks with their requisitions and the naked men, women, and children waiting to take their death showers? Who could take the measure of modern times that promoted the genius of machines and machine-like behavior? Who could hold those euphemisms—"resettlement," "evacuation"—in his or her mouth and not choke? Perhaps what the world needed was not philosophy but a new Bible.

Despite her doubts—or because of them—she persevered as a free person is supposed to persevere. She touched on the obedience that the Jews were locked into, their filling out the endless paperwork the Nazis required of them, their standing in the lines that took them to their deaths. Many Jews howled at Hannah's written touch. They felt she was unfair, unfeeling, and little better than a traitor. Despite her intelligence, she was naïve. There could be no qualifiers to the hideous, larger truth. But for Hannah, who was trained to consider the whole topography of truth and was steeped in the modern literature of desperation, there were such qualifiers, just as Eichmann had a grotesque, comic side as he sat there and clarified points of order about how he did his job. He was eager to speak and explain. He wanted to set the record straight. He may have been acting, putting on a performance while inwardly baying at the most horrendous of moons. To assert his enthusiasm as a Nazi would have been very bad form. Yet there he was, quite composed, ready to argue some peccadillo about the murderous protocols. He would, as they say in New York, "do anything to save his own skin." His testimony may have been nothing but lies but it still was testimony. He had been there. No one argued that point.

She thinks about this Eichmann as a representative of the human race. To assume that any given person has a conscience is a big assumption. To assume that the conscience has some depth and is something more than petty self-righteousness is a bigger assumption. The endeavor of philosophy, her life's endeavor, is to examine assumptions. Her husband, who is a living representative of the Socratic tradition, does that each day—one of many reasons why she loves him. His conscience is not so much pure as stalwart and restless. Like Jaspers, he grasps how much philosophy's posing of questions can matter. People need philosophy, its rigor and scope, but they don't know they need it.

Sometimes as she sat in that courtroom in Jerusalem she felt that she would explode with irony—a terrible feeling. The man in the dock was, as Americans put it, "a loser." He could not *think*; he could only follow directions or register his displeasure with those who didn't follow directions. He was not the person who should have been sitting there. Despite all the deaths he had orchestrated she felt that he was not the main act but an afterward. The horrific inspiration the Germans had derived did not emanate from this man who seemed in his vacant, responsible way nothing so much as narrowly ambitious. The enormous effort of the trial was spent on a hateful nothing.

But no—the trial (and she can't help but think of Kafka) showed what the word *conscience* could be. In that sense those who excoriated her were wrong-headed. To live in a world without conscience was unbearable. To say that one conscience equaled another was foolish. As Eichmann showed too well, one conscience did not equal another. The scales were broken. Or they never worked to begin with. Kafka would have understood.

To say, "This is wrong" is as crucial as anything a human being can do. She gave examples in *Eichmann in Jerusalem* of people who paid with their lives for having a conscience. It was not complicated: the Third Reich was a nightmare they had to oppose. And yet she understands how easy rationalizing can be. Life is an extenuating habit. One Jew tells another Jew that things will be okay. Not all the rumors are bad. One Nazi tells another Nazi that a job must be done. There is honor. There is duty. There is the Fatherland. There is the Special German Way. Each abstraction is palpable. One German tells another German that the *Führer* knows what he is doing. "He has a plan." She thinks of the story about the German woman at the end of the war saying, "The Russians will never get us. The *Führer* will never permit it. Much sooner he will gas us." To which Hannah added: "There should have been one more voice, preferably a female one, which, sighing heavily, replied: And now all that good, expensive gas has been wasted on the Jews!"

Like more than a few of her Jewish brethren, Hannah could have had a career as a comic or a writer of what has been called "black humor." It comes with the burdensome territory inhabited by Job and Abraham and Sarah and Rachel, but she refuses to stay in that territory, much less indulge it. She is clear about being a Jew first and last but the identity doesn't buoy her. What buoys her is the patient, and, more likely than not, irritating quest for the truth of any small or large matter. What buoys her are the crowded streets of New York where people jostle each other, exchange greetings, gossip, wrangle, and mutter to themselves in various languages. The republic has no great task. Or its great task is to respect each person walking along Broadway, which is up to each citizen who constitutes the republic.

Again, she stands outside a record store and listens. Some young men with British voices are shout-singing about love. "Help!" Sweet yet ardent, the word throbs with imploring warmth. She nods as if to acknowledge this most basic of human pleas. Something always is rising from the demiurge's ashes. You wouldn't want to live forever—but you would.

James Jesus Angleton

WHAT HE COULDN'T FATHOM—and he was a great fathomer—about his fellow Americans was their ignorance. He realized it was their pleasure and almost a right and that, in a sense, he was, as an employee of the Central Intelligence Agency, not only defending that right but indulging it. They could waltz through their oblivious, happiness-pursuing lives and never know how much malign mischief skulked two steps behind them. He was protecting them, tucking them in each nationally secure night while mumbling a prayer to the rogue assets of counterintelligence. Yet beyond the un-God-given, American freedom to go off somewhere and fuck up, he would have had a hard time defining who and what he was defending. The nation at large was full of disagreeable people he wouldn't be caught dead with. Negroes? Homosexuals? There were some Jews at Yale but they weren't people you'd want to meet socially, even to someone, such as he, whose mother was Mexican. They were smart of course but they were leftists usually or worse. You wouldn't trust them and, in its warped way, his world revolved around trust.

"Trust" wasn't a word anyone used much because it was a soft word, and everything in his Right-versus-Wrong, Them-against-Us world, the lies, coups, assassinations, and suitcases filled with cash, was an ultimatum. He sat in an office in suburban Virginia where he had nothing more fearsome to look at than the sky and a parking lot, but at the other end of whatever scenario was being played out far off in an alley or car or prison, something very unpleasant could be happening. His life wasn't on the line but that didn't take the edge off. He neither gloated nor lost sleep. It was, after all, a *cold* war. His job was to hoard secrets and function. How those two demands were supposed to correlate was anyone's guess.

The danger of the enterprise wasn't voyeurism on his part. His imagination, at least when he was young, had tended to go to modernist places like the lyrical, lower-case leaps of e. e. cummings or the history-plundering of Ezra Pound. Like the poets, he enjoyed taking worlds apart and reassembling them. As was often the case with poets and their literary spats, he needed an enemy to help define himself and was fortunate to have such a one as the ponderous Union of Soviet Socialist Republics. He'd never been to Moscow or Stalingrad but the physical locations were irrelevant. The USSR was opposite to America and he was, constitutionally, an opponent.

As a word and a notion, *trust* sounded like something from a nineteenth-century essay where a humming, well-barbered gentleman writer adumbrated a coherent moral landscape, detailing the shortcomings and excellences then summing matters up with some commodious maxim about how worthless human life was without trust. He could only envy such a person his naiveté. It must have been simpler to live back then and have the seemingly unassailable foundation of God on which to rest your spirit and occasional insight. During the American Civil War, both sides had leaned on God for justification. He appreciated the paradox of enemies playing the same trump.

The notion of leaning on Vladimir Lenin, however, made him ill. Lenin, after all, was a mere man. So, in moments he preferred not to think about, was Angleton. He'd befriended the Soviet agent Kim Philby, drank with him, swapped stories, told him who knew what secrets, and caused who knew what grief. He'd trusted Philby or, amazingly enough, he'd never much thought about not trusting him. Philby was upper-class British. That was something to be trusted in its own right. How embarrassing that all the clichés about Americans looking up to proper Brits were true. What made his lack of professional caution worse was that Angleton had gone to school in England. He should have known. Yet when Philby was fingered, Angleton refused to believe it. Philby couldn't be a spy. The reason was, well, he just couldn't be.

By anyone's standards, the twentieth was a harsh century, not only on account of the wars and genocides but on account of the ruination of personal relationships wrought by politics and ideology, the loss of simple humanity. There had been betrayers and traitors throughout history but the consequences seemed steeper in modern times. The United States and the Soviet Union weren't engaged in a grudge match like Trojans and Greeks, or a difference about an established institution like the American North and South. They were engaged in a rivalry about how to organize life on earth. When Philby went over to the Soviets, he as much as admitted he did not agree with how the West organized life. Or he despised the West so much, he did not care. Or he liked the thrills of duplicity and manipulating people. Or all those motives applied to him.

The field of intelligence, to say nothing of Angleton's specialty, counterespionage, was like an uncontrollable novel in which characters continually questioned one another's behaviors and attitudes. Points of view multiplied like amoebas. As in Henry James, one action could result in days, months, and years of probing, exhaustive, and less-than-conclusive analysis. Though he would have rejected the literary analogy, Angleton's job was to be in charge of the characters. Philby's treachery was more painful because of that. Angleton's supreme trust in himself had been violated. For any egotist, that was a long fall off an important cliff. Of course, the fall was secret and the cliff was secret. That was how Angleton's world worked. If something wound up in the newspapers such as the day Philby walked into the Soviet embassy in Beirut, it was only the final chapter of a lengthy and convoluted drama. The crucial actions already had occurred, much like in a James novel where a sigh or glance signaled the demise of vast yet finite complications.

Angleton's confederates knew he had trusted Philby. No doubt they sniggered about his lapse. He had been gulled, snookered, taken in, duped, and knew they knew. That too was like a novel. People took advantage of other people. People spoke behind people's backs. The omniscient narrator recorded it all. Angleton might have protested that what Philby did was not fair. That, however, would have branded Angleton as one of those innocents he despised. The world Angleton had chosen to enter was compounded of treachery. It was his job to see through people and not fog his vision with feeling.

Sometimes when he thought about Philby—and he thought often about Philby after Philby went over—he sensed that it took one to know one. Such a thought did not appall him but it did not please him either. Through the landscape of the Cold War, a river ran with Good on one side and Bad on the other. Anything could be done on the side of the Good because routinely anything was done on the side of the Bad. Given the circumstances, a person could indulge in something like visceral rationalization. Any means were justified and anything could happen. The river was clearly demarcated—the mindboggling, degenerate Soviets didn't even believe in God—but a person could lose perspective in the long-standing heat of the fray.

Imagine, for a moment, Harold Wilson, the prime minister of the United Kingdom, as a KGB agent. Angleton served it up as a truth to anyone who would listen. It was not that big a leap. Wilson represented Labour. They were all semi-Reds. He had known a card-carrying communist or two. There was nothing wrong with guilt by association; people were judged by the company they kept. How else were you to know someone? You could not peer into a person's soul, particularly in an irreligious age. You could bug the person's phone and premises and even 10 Downing Street. You could insinuate. You could make charges. You could say you cannot reveal what your sources are. You could stress the gravity of the situation.

But there was no gravity. That was the drastic rub. Anything could be considered as truth. Anything could be plausible. In that sense there was something medieval about Angleton's CIA work. How many angels can dance on the head of a pin was an unanswerable yet germane question. It sounded the fantastic depths of intelligibility. Once you have a premise, you have a game.

If someone once betrays you, it makes sense to feel that others will betray you. James Jesus Angleton did not know James Harold

Wilson. That did not matter. And the consequences of the prime minister being a KGB agent did not seem that extraordinary. The Brits were hard to figure out; Philby had turned out to be very hard to figure out. The Beatles made no sense to anyone who had grown up on Glenn Miller. The clothes on Carnaby Street were not made for real people. The model known as Twiggy did not seem like a woman. Without an empire to run, the Brits had lost their way. You lose your power and you wind up believing in James Bond.

The wilderness of mirrors shows whatever the viewer wants to see. So Angleton was suspected by a CIA colleague of being a KGB agent. If he was not, his accusations about the British prime minister caused so much consternation that he might as well have been. Accusations have a way of doing that. Angleton felt that Lee Harvey Oswald was a KGB agent. Or that Oswald was set up so as to seem to have killed the president. Or that he was not a KGB agent—not everyone who spent time in Russia was a KGB agent. Oswald also was CIA. He may have been a double agent, though no one knew which side he was betraying. He could have been betraying both sides. He had enough anger, disgruntlement, and imagination to go around. If any one person did know the truth or still knew, that person was not talking, because such people only talk to one another. Or they do not talk to anyone. Or there is no truth; there is only disinformation heaped upon disinformation. All the mirrors are set at angles.

Back in the 1960s when banners were in fashion, the Agency could have participated too: Making the World Safe Through Paranoia. Laugh if you will. Didn't you wonder about Harold Wilson, him smoking that stupid, I'm-an-intellectual pipe and acting as if he respected capitalism? He could have danced on the large head of a nefarious plot.

Laugh if you will, but Angleton did not. After the fact, after the Eastern bloc no longer was a bloc and the Union was no longer a union, it was easy to laugh. Even the latter-day president of Russia, an espionage pro, told spy jokes at Russia's expense. But in the days of Angleton, of the Cuban Missile Crisis and the U-2 incident and the endless Red menace, none of this was funny. And to the millions on the other side, it was not funny either. Like everyone else, Angleton saw the newspapers with the faces of the Hungarian freedom fighters.

Those pictures pained him. He had to do something. Every day, that burned inside of him: he had to do something. Yet he was one of those men who played chess against himself: every move provoking a counter-move, every belief meeting disbelief, gradually reaching a stalemate whose only solution lay in the blank embrace of alcohol. He believed in the crusade against communism yet disbelieved crucial defectors and refused to follow up on leads they supplied, convinced those leads were lies. They were not. Numerous Soviet spies continued spying thanks to the disbelief of James Jesus Angleton. This was one reason he eventually would be fired. Another was that he never caught a spy nor did he uncover the mole he believed to be in the CIA. He did sow more paranoia and hard feeling.

The CIA, as it evolved after World War Two, was a new principality within the borders of the USA. Stoked by fear of the Reds, the Company, as it came to be blandly called, had a life of its own. The Company worked in the service of the nation, but such a hermetic entity was bound to create its own agenda. People there—like Angleton—knew about matters no one else knew about. The lawmakers and even the president who supposedly oversaw those matters were quaint festoons of democracy.

Given the perspective that intelligence work demanded—cautious on one hand and risky on the other—a person doing such work could get his head turned around. A person could run amok with speculation yet talk a seemingly sane game.

The Company and its employees existed in historical time but were proponents of anti-history, a no-place of no speeches, no elections, no public debates. Everything happened on the sly, in the dark, under cover. Airless and sunless, anti-history was the province of manipulation and disinformation. Everything, accordingly, was open to doubt, making way for a metaphysical wonderland. Once a nation gave itself to anti-history, it no longer was a nation in the sense of a public civic identity but more like a dynamic charade. The juggernaut of American virtue could not exist without its enemies. Which came first—the juggernaut or the enemies?—was a question that in the heat of the Cold War did not bear asking. The Soviet Union, after all, was the juggernaut of its own brand of virtue and disinformation.

Angleton's job was to create meaning out of the chaos of intelligence, a job that God could not do, which may have been why it appealed so deeply to someone whose middle name was Jesus. It was a scholar's job in some senses—the assiduousness, the linking of darkness with opacity, the belief that one mind could put together what had been randomly created by many minds. Those tangles could divulge clues. Those clues could unmask plots. Those plots could end the known world. Angleton sat at his desk and pondered.

How alone men can be! When he wasn't communing with the anxieties of the free world, Angleton sequestered himself in the cellar of his house, where he fashioned custom jewelry and leather belts, or he took off for some solo fly-fishing in northern Wisconsin.

His situation was extreme but he was representative, too. The biological dividing line was basic: men's bodies do not sustain future lives. Given, then, their inherent shortsightedness—no generations are brooding inside of them—how men sustain themselves may well be both violent and arcane. Kings, nation-states, and political notions speak, among other matters, for the awful lacking within men. Men are not to blame for that (though women were blamed by men for their bodies, right from the Judeo-Christian start) but to make a virtue of non-receptivity seems badly out of sync with the fecund whole of life. Though he was dealing with the massive complexity of two competing economic and political systems and their myriad repercussions, Angleton was in a tunnel. He looked very hard and worked very hard but he was in a tunnel that was literally man-made.

Those who are protecting others may not protect themselves. Or they may protect themselves in recondite ways that are of no help to anyone. Angleton was prone to believe there was a vast conspiracy organized by the communists. In fact, there were communist conspiracies but how vast they were was another story. Unified mental concepts break down over time and are replaced by bits and pieces. The *Internationale* becomes national and then merely personal. Mental matter, like physical matter, ossifies and decays. Angleton sits at a restaurant in Georgetown and downs martini after martini while trying to unravel the secrets of many hidden minds. He orders another double. At night he might go through a fifth of bourbon and a bottle of wine. He could, as men like to say, drink anybody under the table.

In its odd, unhappy way, his obsessive endeavor was reassuring. Nations are small, daily fears writ large. Security is the obverse of fear and fear is unlikely to disappear unless a concerted spiritual effort is made. To make a fetish of security is to promote insecurity. When Angleton bridled at civilian interference from the nation's elected officials, it seemed ridiculous in one way—they were the elected officials, not he—but understandable in another. If the heart of the nation was security/insecurity then the CIA was the true nation within the nation, a secret in the way the soul is secret in the body. Any Gnostic would tell you that the body is just a husk.

So Angleton, the soul saver, stashed secret documents in safes and vaults. Since the CIA dealt in secrets, it made sense for a CIA employee to create secrets within secrets, to cocoon the fears. At no moment did he think he was anything less than wholly rational. When he assumed that every defector was a KGB plant; when he sought to prove that Oswald was a KGB agent; when he believed that Harold Wilson was working for the Soviets; when he suspected Henry Kissinger—the list goes on and starts to seem comic—did he believe he was anything less than rational? Men have that right. Women, according to them, are the irrational ones. If you know how to structure your fears, you are reasonable.

Of all the poets, the great poet of fragments, T. S. Eliot, appealed the most to Angleton. In all likelihood, very few of his cronies at the CIA spent what spare time they had rereading *Four Quartets*. It isn't hard to see why Eliot would make soul sense to Angleton. Perhaps no modern poet was as in touch with ghosts as Eliot was. In Eliot's poetry, life on earth was a vast haunting. There was no overarching conspiracy to the haunting, hence the fragments. The pieces dangled in the ether—voices, images, mottoes, scriptures, human incidents, places—and never settled. To try to make the pieces settle would be an act of violence. One implication of his poetry is that whatever spiritual wisdom humans may attain is connected to that acceptance. You cannot force order. The river of life is too enormous. Eliot had grown up in the heart of America near to the Mississippi and never forgot that "strong brown god." Like Angleton, that god was "intractable."

Angleton hailed from Idaho. When he died he was eulogized by one of Idaho's senators as "the very symbol of the mysterious world of counterintelligence." It is a human prerogative to wish that historical circumstances would be different from what they are. Any person, in his or her way, may try to effect that change. When wishes turn into actions, we may embrace, as many a former ideologue could testify, what may destroy us. Eliot embraced mystery and was sustained. Angleton embraced a very different mystery and was, in effect, destroyed. The "mysterious world" he lived in was based on duplicity. That vicious fact could eat a person alive.

Who knows how many dreams and nightmares of Angleton's featured his onetime friend Kim Philby? Having been betrayed, he must have vowed never to be betrayed again. The next sentence to write is that "He betrayed himself" but no one can write that sentence. That sentence belongs to the pieces dangling in the ether, the intuitive insubstantialities of poems that attracted Angleton with their oblique, inveigling intelligence.

PHILIP BERRIGAN

I saw the Beast the other day. I see the Beast every day. There's nothing special about the Beast. He wears a suit and tie. He wears a uniform. He goes about his business. And he chews you up. You may not realize it, the chewing is so quiet, very impressive in its way—the chewing. It's like the weather, just something that's there. You die and you don't even know. How smooth is that?

PHILIP WAS A QUESTIONER. The questions never were about "why." The margins of God's mystery more than encompassed "why." It was "how" that was crucial. How to oppose and be positive at the same time? How to not despair? How to make spirit credible? How to protest what everyone accepted as the given state of affairs? How to engage violence without giving oneself over to violence? How to respect authority—the church and otherwise—but not be buried by it?

A pilgrim, every person of faith being a pilgrim, started with the example of Christ, which was not so much an example as an incitement. Unless a person was incited by Christ, you weren't receiving what Christ had to give. Unfortunately the incitement might ruin a person's habitual, orderly life. Christ, of course, acknowledged that ruination. His good news was trouble. If going to prison showed ruination, then Philip Berrigan's life was ruined many times. Like many a political prisoner in the twentieth century, he could have written a book called *My Prisons.* Over a decade for Philip Berrigan: Danbury, Lewisburg, Hagerstown, Peterson. Over three thousand days, up at 7:30, work detail all day, inmate count at 5:30; as prisoners put it, he knew the inside. He knew the determination needed to go from one faceless day to another, the lassitude, the small and large brutalities, the feeling of being lost to the world. At the age of seventy-six, having invaded yet another government weapons facility, he was sentenced to thirty months for "malicious destruction of property and conspiracy to maliciously destroy property." He knew too well what he was getting into.

Prison is the Beast's right hand. War is his left.

When his mother was asked about her law-breaking son, she replied that he hadn't broken any of God's laws.

Life on earth is the breaking of God's laws. Between what should be and what is a grand canyon exists. Is it too symbolic that one of America's main sights is a chasm? Philip understood the value of symbols. His pouring blood on the nose cones of nuclear warheads and hammering them as if to make them into plowshares were symbols. From a practical point of view those actions accomplished nothing. One war followed another. The missiles (those "hellish eggs" in the words of Philip's brother, Daniel Berrigan) remained in their silos ready to be used. What emerged, however, from the actions were the questions Philip treasured. What if the politics that got written about each day and talked about each night by well-groomed newscasters, pundits, and politicians themselves was nothing more than get-along exigency? What if the practical viewpoint—what had to be done—was nothing more than the fear of stepping out of line? What if the line was murderous? What if *Realpolitik* wasn't realistic at all? What if common sense was death-in-life, a slow suffocation of feeling? How many spiritual people—ascetics, mendicants, God's holy fools, prophets—had been shown the door in modern times as impractical? How had spirit been removed to a harmless outer orbit? Why didn't people understand how terrible a spiritless life was?

Those, like Philip and his cohorts, who refused Caesar were to be scorned and despised but that was nothing new. What, after all, had Christ received? Nor were religions necessarily spiritual. The priorities were plain: church on Sunday, the rest of the week for power's prerogatives. As for salvation, it could be considered money laid aside in a conscience-saving, anxiety-allaying bank account called Heaven.

The actions that Philip helped to orchestrate took a lot of time and planning. The approved courses of action would have been simpler—write letters to the editor, man a picket line, give a sermon. Those actions could placate conscience. They were, in their ways, honorable. Philip, however, was implacable. There was no checking off an action and moving on in one's busy day. God's word came first. The discussion ended there. Or there was no discussion because there was nothing to discuss. You acted from the pit of your soul or you didn't. And your soul was there as long as your body was.

It wasn't hard on the inside to collect adages. *Don't trust anyone who hasn't done time. People who get in the way are going to be run over. A Judas snitch is born every minute. A conscience is a luxury.*

These were street wisdom, cynical wisdom, bent wisdom, loser wisdom. They spoke to the hard experience that wore a person down to nothing.

In the face of those adages the Bible that Philip cited each day is right now, not something in the buried past. If you grasp that, you may feel, like Philip, a great urgency. Our time here is short. We eat and drink each day and have a thousand thoughts, but our time here is short.

In 1967 Robert McNamara, the then Secretary of Defense, informed Lyndon Johnson that the war in Vietnam was not a winnable war. US troops left in 1973.

Do the math.

Philip Berrigan was a minister of peace. Or was he? Shouldn't he have been on an extended spiritual retreat building up reserves of sagacious calm? Why did he participate in futile actions in the world? The world—armies, defense contractors, patriots—was incorrigible. He knew that. He ticked people off. If you ticked people off, you weren't contributing to peace. You were building more animus, more violence. He saw the photo of the trooper looking at his brother Dan when Dan was freed from jail for the Catonsville action. The man's face was pure, sneering disgust. Wouldn't more peace occur by sitting down and talking with that man? He was human, too.

You did time and you did talk to people. The guards didn't tend to talk. They knew whom they served. The prisoners, however, didn't know. Even the ones with the likes of "Satan" tattooed on their arms weren't sure. Brimming with swagger and bluster, they despaired and pretended they didn't despair. They prided themselves on their anger. No one was going to fool them. Everyone in this world had fooled them but no one was going to fool them. Philip talked with them and listened to them. A few listened to him, his hustle about Jesus and God. When Philip asked a fellow prisoner what the man saw inside of himself, there often was a silence.

I see shit. I see death. I see darkness. I see what's none of your damn priest business.

Philip continued to listen. He prayed for them. That may have been the hardest thing to explain—what prayer was. It seemed the biggest hustle of all, some mumbo jumbo that made nothing happen. It seemed like a little kid wishing for a Christmas present. Grown men didn't wish. They made things happen. Modern times were about making things happen. You pressed buttons and switches. Gears moved. Engines started. Prayer didn't seem to do anything.

He tried to explain. Prayer was a way of communicating between what was small and what was vast. A person's life was small. All that a person did not understand was vast. What a person intuited, even a sleepless person lying on a prison bunk, was vast. Prayer honored that.

You could imagine prisoners listening to him and walking away, shaking their heads. "What was Father Phil talking about?" some of them asked one another. Together, they tried to think it over. What was he talking about? God and peace and the "waste of it."

Meanwhile, bombs falling on cities and towns and hamlets. Meanwhile, people dying by the thousands, people without guns, children and old women and old men dying and mothers holding babies, their skin turning to jelly, their bodies exploded, their souls gone into nothingness, their screams rendered empty, their quick, beautiful eyes vanquished.

No more of these days for you. No more.

One deity Philip often invoked was Mars. The pagans acknowledged a god of war as part of their polytheistic landscape. They treasured their honor and were prepared to kill or be killed. Some of the prisoners Philip met were like that—ready to die over what seemed a trifle. Some would die. Yet every life should be something more than a witless morsel offered up to Mars, or so Philip believed. Every life must be sacred. There could be no other way for a Christian, but *sacred* was a hard word to use. Human beings seemed in their scratching, complaining, ever-ingesting way to be distinctly un-sacred. To form a bridge between the divine, the miraculous force that informed the earth and heavens, and the workaday confusion of mortals was stern work. It might seem at first, and even at a longer glance, to be impossible work.

It was that difficulty that attracted Philip, who came from a hardscrabble background, both physically and emotionally. His father had been remote, his mother persevering; the farm on which the family had lived—parents and six boys—demanded ceaseless labor for negligible gain. Neither the pastels of beauty nor the tactful nods of subtlety had counted. There was only survival garnished with his father's cold, proud turmoil and his mother's resolute love. It was an upbringing that could impel a young man to the grandeur and wisdom of the Church. There had to be more to this world than the starved bones of willfulness.

The consolations of religion separated Philip from his fellow priests. They took and gave and were more or less healed in the process. They achieved the mild stasis of identity. They could lay their heads on the pillow of infinite surmise and slumber peacefully. God was in His heaven. For Philip, however, there was no stasis. Inside of him the fuse of justice burned and refused to accede to any larger, more sanguine cause. Salvation was a supreme gift, but life on earth remained mired in some very deep ruts, war being a major one. Philip, who was an idealist with a practical vengeance, a down-to-earth symbolist, took the ruts personally. As an immigrant haven, America was always mixing up its human categories. Philip—German/Irish, rural/urban, pacifist/warrior—was a prime example.

When he stood, in one of his first anti-war actions, tossing draft files into a fire, he seemed at once at peace and about to split open with grief. He was performing an exorcism that took calm, nerve, and faith. If not many people, either inside or outside the church, understood what he was doing that was irrelevant. Someone had to take upon himself the casting out of evil. You could say such a person was imperious, stubborn, and poorly grounded in the tactics of persuasion. Philip wouldn't necessarily have disagreed with you. He also wouldn't have stopped. The task was too urgent. Inside the formal edifice of religion lay the promptings of spirit.

The unhappy truth was that Christ, about whom such an endless hullaballoo was raised, was a radical not a reformer. Once a person took to heart the message of Christ then all was possible because all was impossible—and yet it clearly wasn't. Christ's story was one of impossibility and despair—and yet. That was what made it the strongest story, stronger even than the stories of wars, of *The Iliad* or *War and Peace*. Perhaps that was what the author of *War and Peace* had come to grasp in his devout later days. For his part, Philip grasped it quite early. In World War II he had calculated artillery fire, guarded Nazi prisoners, and taken part in the nightmare known as the Battle of the Bulge. He had experienced first-hand the sickening reality of war. He, too, had been property of the State.

As a Josephite, an order organized in the nineteenth century as a "Negro apostolate," Philip ministered to blacks in Baltimore, Maryland. While most white people were following the whirligig of modernity—all the good things money increasingly could buy—Philip spoke each day to people who wondered how long the prejudice would go on, where their next meal was coming from, and how their children could better themselves in a world that detested them. His parishioners faced not just one wall but an interlocking series of walls. Hate, indifference, contempt, complacency; all the behaviors summed up in the word "racism" formed a powerful mortar.

More than once the walls had tumbled down; they could tumble down again. Though the Church had many walls of its own, the Church could nurture the spirit to bring the walls down. Philip recognized the paradox but was not held by it. If anything, the paradox emboldened him. In facing the devastation of war, he was, as a true disciple of Christ, in a perfect place. He could draw on the spirit and forthrightly enact the spirit. Cardinal Spellman might insist the Vietnam War was "Christ's war," but Philip Berrigan owed the cardinal no apology. He could accept the perennial promise the Church offered and go forward with that promise.

What Philip and others did was to connect the dots between racism, permanent war in the name of defense, daily violence, and the narcotic of the materialist life. The dots weren't very far apart. Philip had seen how black soldiers were treated in World War Two. He'd done basic training in the South and had seen the shacks and the segregated facilities for everything, including the worship of God. The racism and grief he saw in Baltimore were palpable, but the dot that was the "military-industrial complex" was removed from public purview and seemed to have its own life. In a perverse way, the presence Dwight Eisenhower had called attention to in his Farewell Address to the Nation, was part of "progress": more sophisticated weapons, deadlier weapons, and weapons heretofore undreamed of. One of the prime American mottoes was "You can't stop progress." Every day brought something new in the news. Who was he to argue with that?

Only someone determined to go to the human heart of the matter, someone neither amused nor captivated by progress, would argue with that. One large dilemma for such a person lay in finding a credible home amid the brisk self-satisfaction. Philip Berrigan's outlook was based on spiritual perceptions while the compounded reality confronting him was technological, moneyed, patriotic, scientific, and mediated by a thousand chiding editorials. A mere dwarfed human life took place in some rooms in a row house in Baltimore—or in a prison cell. It didn't take place on some justice-hungering, spiritual map.

But—and that was the imitation of Christ made palpable—it did.

At certain junctures—love and death being two main ones—words fall apart. We reside in words and go forth each day as we speak with one another, but the words, even the divinely inspired ones, even prayers, can only go so far. That isn't to disparage language. It is to feel the pressing inwardness of being human, that which cannot be expressed in words.

More often than not that pressure is violent: after the harsh words and arguments come grudges, fights, thefts, beatings, retaliations, vendettas, feuds, persecutions, murders, executions, wars, and genocides. As a list of miseries, this could be expanded upon almost endlessly. In his years in America's federal penitentiaries Philip listened to many testimonies from his fellow prisoners: one hell led to a worse one.

Death exacts finality; love demands proofs. For Philip, the deaths brought about by nation-states did not trump the proofs of love but they cast a baleful shadow. If most people dismissed the shadow, asserting that conventional wars had to be fought and that nuclear weapons would never be used, he was not most people. *Never* was for him a foolish word. So was the phrase *had to*. The Bible told the truth: human beings tended to be Pharisees. They saw what they wanted to see, what made them comfortable. They saw in Christ a ragged troublemaker. Circumstances changed but socialized viewpoints didn't.

Christ preached but he performed actions, too. Miracles were symbols of the incredible made credible. They showed how narrow the human mind was and how wide the divine. Protesting the mores of violence wasn't enough. Violence in all its potentiality—the arsenals and files—had to be confronted.

In taking on the reality of the State, Philip was tilting at a massive, vindictive windmill. If his actions seemed grimly quixotic, as each action turned into another prison sentence, the notion of efficacy had to be examined in light of that integrity called "conscience." Conscience made a human being into a human being: the texts, ancient and modern, agreed on that. The struggle that often went into forging a conscience took a degree of courage, perhaps a powerful degree.

Philip's conscience was fierce—not violent but fierce. Spiritual fire had to oppose military fire. People like the Berrigan brothers and those who came to be known as the Catonsville Nine and the Plowshares Eight were not unknown in American history; the Abolitionists preceded them by over a hundred years. Slavery had been part of that world's order. Southern ministers cited Scripture to buttress their case. Those who opposed slavery and resorted to unruly tactics—burning the Constitution in public—were labeled hooligans. When, upon arresting Philip Berrigan, a police officer complained that he would have to change his religion, he was speaking for many Northern churchgoers in the decades before the Civil War. They did not share in the act of imagination that put some in the intolerable place of those slaves. Igniting the conscience often took an act of imagination. Philip's imagination ran to a kind of testifying theater. Like any act of imagination, there was no right or wrong therein. The words that accompanied and explained the act were there, too, but the central concern was the act.

There is a painting by Pieter Brueghel the Elder entitled "The Blind Leading the Blind" that shows a group of blind people linked together. The leader of the group falls into a hole. The man behind the leader begins to fall, his face pure, awful terror. All the others will fall, too. "Can the blind lead the blind?" Christ asked. "Will they not both fall into the ditch?"

Citizens amassed bank accounts, homes, automobiles, wardrobes, and, of course, weapons, endless numbers of weapons, guns upon guns. So the State amassed endless numbers of weapons to protect its citizens from others with weapons. This amassing made sense. Anyone could see the logic. If you don't stand up … If you don't nip it in the bud … If you don't fight back … If you don't make a preemptive strike … If you let the enemy get ahead of you … If you give an inch … If you don't use the latest technology … If you don't play hardball … If you don't recognize those in authority who know what they are doing, who are acting in your interest ...

Philip had great zest inside him; he was not sacrificing his days for others. Graphically, he chose life over death. He could see what lay behind and what lay ahead. "Yes," the vast human congregation murmurs, "Yes, but ..." Yet for some there is no "but." Peace is an absolute—that it passes understanding was all the more reason to embrace it.

George F. Kennan

H<small>E LOOKS OUT THE TRAIN WINDOW</small> and wonders, Who owns this?

The proletariat.

The peasantry.

The State.

Former aristocrats whose spirit lingers.

Animals.

Explorers.

Shamans.

No one.

He thinks about how Siberia is as much a verb as a noun. To have Siberia as part of a nation's geography is to accept an inherent degree of desolation in the nation's soul. Mischievous children are banished to corners or closets. Adults are banished to a place where the physical and metaphysical merge heartlessly. A retributive cloud hangs over every "antisocial" action but the cloud is a landmass. It does not hover. It exists far away but is not some hypothetical. Nor is it fanciful. Grim and cruel, Siberia is a wicked stepmother. But not wicked, just indifferent earth.

Swaddled like an infant in various layers of indeterminate cloth, the man across from him in the railway car grunts. His age, too, is indeterminate. Time has creased and weathered him. He appears to have been left out-of-doors in all seasons. Or he has been dug up from a peat bog. Or he is part tree. The man grunts again then snorts. He smells ripe. A human barnyard is seated opposite the deputy chief of the United States mission in Moscow.

How many days will this journey take? Kennan realizes he has asked the question aloud. Sometimes his thoughts are so vivid that happens. He has spoken in Russian.

"Not many," the man replies.

If the people take on some degree of the abundance of time that the land possesses, they need not be bothered by the reckoning of years. So the judgments meted out to the people over the past centuries by czars and commissars—ten years, twenty years, thirty years—mocked a puny lifetime and saluted the brooding, all-devouring land. All power to the tundra, steppe, and forest!

Consigned to an actual oblivion, the criminals and political prisoners lived or they perished or they lived and eventually perished. *House of the Dead* in Fyodor Dostoevsky's accurate phrase. Perhaps the greatest triumph of the spirit is to resist degradation. Russia is the land of Lazarus. Miracles were small matters compared to that perseverance, all that inwardness the external eye could never see. Christ knew that. Dostoevsky knew that Christ knew that.

In the great debate between Tolstoy and Dostoevsky, Kennan prefers Chekhov.

What brought Kennan to Russia was not only imagination but heritage, too. His uncle went to Siberia once upon a time—in the 1890s around the same time that Chekhov took his trip to Sakhalin Island. There is no record of their crossing paths. In the immensity outside the train's window, it is hard to imagine anyone crossing paths.

Another Russian lesson: space conquers time. Time posits movement, but space goes nowhere. Or space grows with the passage of each hour across the endless land. Here you feel it: a human lifetime is nothing.

That's not, as Kennan well knows, an American thought. However obscurely, each pursuer of happiness matters. To be an American and not be an optimist is unpatriotic. Still, to reflect in the manner Kennan loves to reflect is likely to result not in the sunny side of the street but in complaint and lament. The self, which normally in America has an agreeable, definitive glow, turns into something acrid. Yet Kennan is a patriot. He is devoting his life to his career and his career is in the service of his nation. He believes in America, but that may be only because he was born there. Look at the communists who believe in Russia. In the next train compartment are two agents who shadow his every move. Do they believe in what they are doing? Or is it rather that people are animate clay to be shaped by the forces of an era?

Kennan broods about these things. His wife Annelise teases him: "Give humankind a rest, George."

The peasant across from him has fallen asleep. Kennan studies the man's face. Pocks and grooves and scars: he is a map of woe. Yet maybe not. He may have slipped through the nets of history, an immemorial soul dwelling with the rain and wind, one who has kept his head down, said what needed to be said and nothing more.

The history of Russian woe, however, insists. The spirit voices of the dead kulaks, the dead White Russians, the dead counter-revolutionaries, the dead deviationists, the dead Ukrainians, all insist. The categories, even to a so-called specialist like Kennan, seem endless. There has been so much violence, so much death. No one really knows how many have perished in the two world wars. No wonder Kennan has trouble explaining the Union of Soviet Socialist Republics to the diplomats back home. Next to the Russians, Americans, even the ones who consider themselves worldly, are so many rosy-cheeked children. The freedom to live out an individual fate has never been the Russian fate. The modest amount of attention democracy bestows on the individual has never occurred here. The year might as well be 1245 as 1945.

The peasant's head bobs with the rhythm of the train but he doesn't wake up. Anton Chekhov must have seen such a man in a carriage or on a ferry. He must have seen many such men. They filled him with neither hope nor despair. He was able to locate whatever scraps of humanity presented themselves, a gift Kennan envies. Unlike Chekhov, Kennan wants more from people than they can give. To accept people in their sloth and ignorance seems to him to be giving up on people. He upbraids himself but then upbraids himself for upbraiding himself—truly a Protestant vice.

One of the agents looks in the compartment then pretends he is not looking in the compartment which means he looks very intently and immediately moves away. The whole nation is a dumb show, a silent gruesome dance.

Staring out the window, Kennan tries to conjure some congruent vision of his homeland. There is nothing congruent, however, and when, as he is wont to do, he thinks of the United States, he cringes. One of the larger ironies is how freedom leads to triviality. The focus on self-satisfaction, the lack of any sustaining ideals, is bound to do that. He has no desire to be a scold but it is a hard role to resist. Women, he reflects, do much better. Their grievances are more real.

The peasant has awakened. In America there are no peasants. That is part of the difficulty—no simple people who love the soil and have the patience to do small things well; also, no aristocracy to instill manners and taste, just a formless middle, at once complacent and anxious.

Bathlessness. That is what Kennan smells—bathlessness.

He wants to ask the man if he knows who Chekhov is—a stupid impulse, but Kennan's face actually twitches with the question. The peasant notices and appears to regard him skeptically, a tilt of his shaggy head. The Soviet government has made matters plain: foreigners are trouble. An American such as himself might as well have come from the moon.

The train lurches to a halt. There is no station outside—just land without trees, surging, indolent land lying under cloud shadows. The scraps of sunshine feel chill.

"We stop," the peasant says in Russian.

Kennan nods. He feels drowsy, an effect of Russia—soporific.

The peasant looks out the window contentedly. Perhaps he is on his way to his own beheading and is in no hurry. Perhaps he likes to contemplate the laws of physics as he understands them. Perhaps he is saintly. Saints still live in Russia. Modern times have not crowded them out entirely.

The agent looks in again. He is one of those men who always need a shave. His face is gone immediately. The peasant grunts something.

No one ever gets to the bottom of Mother Russia. This pleases, maddens, and inspires Kennan. He has chosen a vocation that demands a degree in divination.

The war is almost over. No Germans ever made their way to this endlessness. What was Hitler thinking when he took on the Soviets? How full of delusion can a human being be, to say nothing of a nation? Kennan shakes his head. The peasant smiles slightly. His teeth are brownish yellow. He makes a soft whistling sound. Perhaps the foreigner who talks to himself is crazy.

Kennan is on his way to visit a steel plant. To what other place would his hosts send him? He has been to Tolstoy's dacha. He has visited a hermitage without hermits. What are the Nazis compared to all the enemies the Soviets have taken on? Religion, privilege, private property, class structure, folk customs, family ties, art: the list staggers even the most revolutionary mind. "Let us undo everything": the theme song of modern times. Also the dirge.

What does he know about a steel plant? *Pig iron, blast furnace, Bessemer process, ore.* He has some vocabulary but he despises the takeover of the human spirit by industrialism, the worship of big and efficient. Machines threw everything out of scale—too fast, too many, too thoughtless. He would change this train for Chekhov's poky, uncomfortable carriage in a moment. Or so he tells himself. As it is, he will offer the requisite compliments when he is told how many metric tons are produced and how many people work there and how without such a plant the Nazis would never have been defeated.

Perhaps the pharaohs were like this too, using up human lives to build monuments. His hosts would reject his idle historical analogy. A steel plant is practical. But the pharaohs thought that preparing their tombs for a trip to the world of the dead was practical.

The peasant pulls out a knife from somewhere on his person while, at the same moment, the agent looks in the compartment. They stare at each other. The peasant takes some sort of sausage out and begins to pare it with his knife. The agent shakes his head.

Are knives permitted? Are sausages permitted? If God is not permitted, is anything truly permitted?

Kennan realizes that the other agent has looked in—Number Two. Do they truly look alike or is it his feeling that they must be alike, that the task subsumes the individual? He is supposed to pay careful attention but his mind has holes and chasms.

The peasant offers Kennan a slice. He demurs but then accepts. There is no telling what he is being offered or how his touchy stomach will respond. He is, however, a guest in the Union of Soviet Socialist Republics. The least he can do is sample a gift of sausage.

Kennan tries to recall how many times he has been up close to the leader of this nation. The image of Stalin as a voracious cat comes into his head. Hordes of mice flee him but to no avail. An ideological satrap, he is rapacious—Tamburlaine in another era. Despite railways, nothing changes.

The train starts up again. The sound of the engine getting under way is that of some female titan in labor. Perhaps the god behind God is Energy. And Energy is Progress, the modern overseer. If there isn't an actual overseer, human beings will invent one.

Pessimist or realist—he needs a gypsy to read his palm and sort him out.

The meat he is consuming is probably pig. It has a smoky yet briny taste. For people who have little, the Russians are generous.

He wishes he could talk to this man across from him. He doesn't want him to be arrested for talking to a foreigner, however. And he may be a secret agent himself, though it's hard to believe the government would go to such lengths as to dress someone up as a nineteenth-century peasant. Or eighteenth-century peasant. He wishes Chekhov were sitting across from him. They could talk about doing good works. He works for the United States government because he believes in good works. No doubt his opposites also believe they are doing good works. The ghost of utopianism, a better world in the making, has confused many.

"Like?" says the peasant.

"Like," George Kennan says in agreement. He enjoys speaking their language. No understanding without language.

"Cow," says the peasant. "Old cow."

"Ah," Kennan mutters.

For a time there is a pleasant silence between the two of them. A strong stomach should go with a foreign posting. Unfortunately, he has ulcers.

"Much land," says the peasant and tips his head toward the window.

There is that smell in the compartment, something fermenting mixed with sweat. Suddenly the air has gotten warm.

"A vast country," he remarks.

Perhaps he is talking to a shaman. The sky hasn't conquered the earth in Siberia. Christianity has come and gone. No doubt it will come again but there is something deeper here, something abiding, something calmly, almost lethargically spiritual.

Trying to get his superiors to understand what they are up against consumes a fair portion of Kennan's being. He counsels that they must be patient and firm in dealing with the Soviets, but patience is not an American virtue. Every four years Americans reinvent themselves in elections, arguing about their identity. A self-created nation has little use for understanding. It is its own dynamic.

He thinks how every vote in the Congress must acknowledge domestic priorities, how virtually every elected representative is an egotist of the first degree. Most of them know as much history as a fourth grader. Some have absolute contempt for history. The United States exists to confound history.

"None of that for us," Kennan says aloud.

"Excuse?" the peasant says.

Kennan switches to Russian. "Just thinking aloud." He tries to smile.

"Yes," the peasant says and pauses. "Some thoughts."

Agent Number Two appears at their door.

The peasant swipes his hand across his mouth to indicate that he wasn't talking but yawning. He closes his eyes.

The agent turns to look at Kennan whose attempted smile has subsided into a vacant stare. The agent scowls. Kennan has the unsettling feeling that the agent is a machine. A scowl is how he comes to life. Now he can properly write a report for his superiors.

Kennan wishes he could talk to the agent about having superiors. Many times he feels that the people reading his reports are little more than stones. Perhaps his agent, who has not walked away from the door, feels the same way. Perhaps they could share the brotherhood of the downtrodden. All power to the bureaucratic proletariat!

What a lot of rubbish Marx dreamed up. Imagine telling an American he is a member of the proletariat. People who have not experienced freedom are bound to replace one tyranny with another.

Agent Number Two opens the door. "Time," he barks to the peasant.

The peasant opens his eyes and shifts on his seat.

"Time," the agent barks again.

Kennan feels something insidious making itself known in his bowels.

The peasant rises, but slowly. He nods courteously to Kennan. He adjusts his cloth cap then moves toward the agent.

"Good day," the peasant says.

"Good day," says Kennan.

The agent says nothing. When he closes the compartment door, he looks darkly at Kennan, this man from America who speaks Russian.

The most prominent product of the Soviet Union is paranoia. This enormous enterprise—with its collective farms, steel mills, banners trumpeting invincibility, its tanks, planes, and agents in black, ugly, ill-fitting shoes—is doomed. All the United States has to do is not be afraid. But modern times have seen paranoia and reality play leapfrog with one another.

He looks out the window at the unchanging landscape: flat, treeless, utterly without consolation, land left over from when God created the earth. "This is a lot of land I didn't need," God might have said. "I didn't have much imagination left." The notion of God confessing pleases Kennan.

How much he wishes he could simply talk to someone. The whole nation is behind glass. He would press his face to the window. He would tap on the glass to draw attention, but he never can talk with anyone. Probably there is a listening device in the railroad car compartment.

Power, fear, power, fear: the train wheels sing those words.

Agent Number One enters and sits opposite Kennan. He proceeds to stare at something on the wall a foot or so to the left of Kennan's head.

"Good day," says Kennan in Russian.

The agent doesn't reply.

"How glad I am to be in the land of Chekhov, a writer whom I revere."

The agent makes a wheezy, exhaling sound. Perhaps a few ounces of dogma are leaving his body. Or he ate some of the peasant's sausage.

"Chekhov, a great Soviet writer," the agent replies.

"A great Russian writer," Kennan corrects while trying to identify from the agent's words where in this endless land he comes from. "Which is your favorite story?"

"Never read him," the agent replies.

Kennan presses himself a bit further back into the seat. It is upholstered in some vague chintz. Soviet style has no style. Style rests in sensibility. Ideology has no time for sensibility. "Bourgeois decadent," "class enemy," "revisionist lackey": the Soviets have a tremendous talent for epithets. To merely admire, to indulge, to appreciate, there is no time for that in the dynamo of modern times. For one piston to rise, another must be denigrated.

And what do sensibility and Chekhov matter beside the toll of the war dead? Russia is dedicated to grief. If any nation on earth can understand tragedy, it is Russia.

The agent has gone back to staring. He has relaxed his neck some. Perhaps he is some sort of mystic who can do this all day. He doesn't need to speak.

"Do you like your line of work?" Kennan asks.

The agent moves his eyes to rest fully on Kennan. A degree of wonder enters his face, a slight upturning of the corners of the mouth.

"Excellent work," he replies. "I help the motherland. I help Stalin our father." He nods his head to confirm the excellence of his profession.

Kennan feels that he, an American diplomat, may run amok very soon. "Diplomat attacks Soviet agent. Diplomat leaps out of moving train. Diplomat steals a knife and stabs himself. Diplomat asks to meet Chekhov." He can see his colleagues shaking their heads. "George always was a bit too temperamental, a bit high-strung, a bit of an artiste for our line of work." George would not be inclined to refute their charges.

In Chekhov's world, people were resolutely people, their foibles were grace notes, their virtues sadly contingent. Everyone in Chekhov squandered his or her feelings but that was the point of life, its pathos and comedy. Earned or unearned, their sorrows sprang from the people around them. Chekhov was the last man of the nineteenth century. This century, as Kennan knows, has gone elsewhere. The political geniuses of the century sought to create this agent staring at nothing. And they succeeded.

Bleak landscape, bleak thoughts.

The agent gets up suddenly.

Kennan realizes that the agent isn't an agent. An agent would never sit like this with him. His agents keep an eye on him. They don't fraternize.

"Who are you?" Kennan asks, but the man is out the door.

It must be the twentieth century. If it were the nineteenth he would be jouncing along in some carriage, fearing that his spleen was about to explode while trading compliments and stories with his fellow passengers. The carriage would smell of liniment, onions, and tobacco smoke. As more than a few officials have told him, they know who the first George Kennan was, an American who traveled in Siberia in the nineteenth century and wrote an esteemed book, *Siberia and Hard Labor*. The title said it all.

But it is the twentieth century that he, George F. Kennan, has been born into, the theater of world wars and ideologies. As much as he desires to be a mere private citizen, a tourist staring at the incomprehensible magnitude outside the train window, he can't be. Total mobilization, total collectivization, total allegiance, total war: History in modern times leaves no one alone.

Did it ever? Is he being nostalgic? Is he yearning for some hypothetical yeomanry, for a mule and forty sanctimonious acres? Is his farm in Gettysburg nothing more than playacting?

A conductor of sorts, at least a man in a uniform, sticks his head into the compartment and pronounces the name of a place Kennan never has heard of.

"I'll get off here," he thinks. "No one will know me. I will know no one. I will explain . . ." But what will he explain? That he has more questions than answers? That he has come to the other side of the earth to learn something he already knew? That he is floating on a lake of horror, millions murdered by a man who might as well have been a direct descendent of Genghis Khan.

The screams of the tortured have been muffled by stone walls and these unyielding distances. And by silence too, the complicity of silence.

Terror—a genuine word.

He does not have to be on this train. He has chosen this. Some obscure romance keeps eating at him, some sense that he will come up against something that will make this suffering come clear and that he can impart to his own people, the gullible, innocent Americans isolated on their ocean-bounded continent.

The train has stopped and someone is knocking against the window, an old woman. She wears a kerchief and the usual non-descript dress, something that once had a color and a pattern. Or it has been made to have barely any color or pattern, in the Soviet style. The woman is waving something in a towel. It must be some local delicacy.

He opens the window. The woman thrusts a small pie into his hands and names an amount.

He smells mushrooms and dill.

"Thank you, stranger," the woman announces when she has pocketed Kennan's money. Then she crosses herself.

He isn't going to starve. While the Jazz Age danced itself silly, millions starved. While F. Scott Fitzgerald considered the lovelorn, yearning lives of flappers and ne'er-do-wells, millions watched their children die and then died with them. Millions died without a comforting priest. Millions stared into a hopeless pit of slogans and denunciations. Nothing more than straw in the historical wind as millions rattled out their last breaths. Millions—the modern number.

The train has resumed. He looks down at the pie. Its edges have been carefully fluted. He finds himself staring, as if he were a child. Something about the wages of human effort seizes him and brings him close to tears. He has not shut the window and the air is cold. Almost reverentially he places the pie on the seat across from him. Eat and be healed. Eat and face another day.

To be an expert on the Soviet Union one has to exercise ruthless compassion. One does not have to be a clairvoyant. This nation isn't going to last forever. As with Rome, the succession of the emperors is shaky. Stalin cannot anoint a son he does not have. As the system wears itself down with its own overbearing emptiness, the contenders for the throne will be little more than minions or criminal connivers. In the scheme of things, this won't take much time. The normalcy of American elections, the heated palaver that lubricates the wheels of democracy, is utterly unreal here. As he has explained more than once to Harriman, the Soviet Union is political but has no politics.

Kennan rises and stretches his arms out then puts his hands at the base of his back and arches backwards. He is stiff. He is tired. He has fooled himself once again into thinking more is there than is there. There is only this unrelenting land.

He walks out into the train corridor. One of the agents—or someone he believes is one of the agents—is smoking a cigarette and gazing out a window. His face is melancholy.

"Homesick?" Kennan asks. Even in another language the word reverberates for him. "I am."

The agent regards Kennan wearily. "You made this trip. We make this trip."

"And how is my peasant friend?"

"There are no peasants in the Soviet Union, only comrades."

"Of course. And we are not speaking to one another."

"Exactly." The agent finishes his cigarette and grinds it out on the train's filthy floor. "You know many things but you know nothing." He heads off toward his compartment.

For a time, Kennan remains in the corridor. He thinks of Chekhov's description of a flogging on Sakhalin Island—the convict's body became bloody, insensate pulp, lash after lash after lash—while the authorities watched complacently. They might as well have been unwrapping a cheese.

The train rumbles and sways. Its motions seem metaphorical but then a great deal of life feels that way. Kennan will return to his compartment and begin drafting in his head yet another paper filled with mettle and foreboding. He will turn up at the new steel-mill city and be suitably feted. His stomach will protest but he will mutter hearty thanks. Then he will lie in a strange bed and wonder how he came to be doing this, wandering the earth in such a semi-purposeful fashion. But he will never get to the heart of anything. His agent is right. Chekhov is right.

Out the window he sees a tree, then a few more. They look like birches. He remembers he has brought a book with him—Gibbon's *Decline and Fall of the Roman Empire*. Perhaps he will quote from it to the next person who occupies his compartment—agent or non-agent, peasant or non-peasant, informer or non-informer. Those sempiternal sentences that take the measure of blood and oratory, lust and stoic calm are a sort of balm. Rise and fall and further fall.

George Harrison

Dead weight, gravity's champions, metal missives of long distance and fascist hatred: the bombs fell on the inoffensive denizens, working-class blokes and lasses, of the port of Liverpool. The endless brick buildings of the nineteenth and earlier centuries collapsed, tumbling in a rush, eager to surrender their proud forms, or fell more slowly like a regret come to light and regarded for some stunned seconds before giving way to brute fact. The sky glowed yellow-orange, hearth of hell, inferno made real, yet formless darkness reached everywhere. Blackout, because the night was not dark enough, blackout in the hearts and minds waiting for the all-clear while every manner of din broke loose—whistling, keening, exploding, droning, screaming, going *bam-bam* and *ack-ack*, and sounds that defied words, sounds that were the dire finale of music, the shards and shouts of explosive death, the world as Liverpool knew it become a nightly conflagration and cacophony, become the true pandemonium, the devil's work.

Waiting in cellars, crypts, vaults, and under anything that offered a semblance of earth-endowed strength, and hoping and praying that whatever was above you would not give way and crush you. How many lay under the bricks, stones, and timbers gasping but sure to die, tormented by pain, thirst, and bitter, bitter grief? How many children died in their parents' arms? How many looked around in the smoky dawn and wondered how long they could endure this? How many wept and could not stop weeping? How many stared out what once was a window at what once was a civil world?

The windows blew out, avenues cratered, downed power lines sizzled and sparked on the macadam, plates shivered in cupboards, dogs whined, bayed, and whimpered, trees caught fire, people caught fire, doors and casements and chairs and rag dolls and love letters and deeds and wills caught fire, flak shells burst, sirens clamored, and women gave birth in hospitals and basements and offices and bedrooms and more than once right in the street where the newborn raised a life-affirming cry for any who stopped to hear it.

"We'll get to the end of this," everyone said, even if they did not believe it, even if they were staring into a pit without any bottom. And if the world of time was the proper and certified domain of loss, of agony hurtling down from the bomber-laden night, they were right. One day followed another like a line of captives on a road in Germany, the men walking and stumbling and falling and rising and walking until stumbling again. And then? And then a guard pointing a gun and firing it.

One day became another because days have nothing better to do, because sense and senselessness have been two-stepping across the human dance floor for millennia and showing no signs of growing tired. "You might as well get used to it," every-one said. They were right and wrong. They kept their heads down. They looked up at the hopeless, innocent sky. They wished the one cup of weak tea they drank each morning could last forever. They stared at what was a window in what was a house on what was a street. They whistled some snatch of a song then halted, appalled.

Peace has never been an adequate word. War's orphan, it has no life of its own. Once you've heard the bombs and smelled the corpses and felt the ashes sifting in the morning breeze, all while watching helplessly without even a weapon in your clammy, civil-ian hands, there is no peace. There are the virtues of hanging on—fortitude, perseverance, even sheer cussed stubbornness. There is memory, unease, desperation, and many blank moments when you realize you are waiting and listening, when you hold your breath, when you feel yourself as a bag of flesh ready to explode, when part of you wishes that would happen. Get it over with.

To fill the emptiness afterwards with what? A house, a marriage, babies, a dog, a car, a radio, a motorbike, a trip to the seaside or London or Scotland, a postal card: *Wish Uncle Jimmy and Aunt Harriet and Cousin Margaret and Brother Fred and little Jane from across the street were here with us.* But they aren't.

Meanwhile, time saws human logs. People begin to reconstruct what has fallen down. They look at their works and say "bet-ter." People doze when the newsreels come on: they already have seen everything. The bombs keep getting bigger. Children sit in classrooms and stare at the maps, the teacher's dress, a dozy fly on the window sill. The great Mass of Knowledge begins its slow avalanche. It is like being pleasantly smothered. The children ci-pher sums, geographies, grammars. There is the agreeable hum of

Things Making Sense. But there is plenty that doesn't make sense and that must be taken on Faith. However battered, England is Faith. But beyond Faith there is luck, accident, coincidence, fate, a whole medley of softly spoken words that the children try to overhear.

The children play in the ruins: cowboys and Indians, RAF and Luftwaffe, cops and robbers. They make wild sounds and point their fingers like guns. They pick up bits of rubble and throw them at one another, hide out amid piles of debris, squat beside shattered walls, peer into still gaping holes. It's a wonderland of sorts, an unbelievable landscape they make believable.

The war made this. Sometimes a child goes off by him- or herself and tells inward stories about what happened. Sometimes a child looks up at the pleasant, empty sky and looks hard for the planes. Sometimes a child listens for that sound that the older people talk about—the metal thunder. The sky is silent, though, and after a while it's time to go home to a little room that the child shares with a sibling and a thin blanket and the cold that is cold but not as cold as it was in the war because nothing that came later compares to the war. The child nods when the word comes up, a childhood spent nodding.

One of the school courses is drawing architectural details— cornices, pediments, ogees, oriels—the ornate, strangely named miscellany of the grand past. For most of the children, the attempted precision is both tedious and pointless. But for others, the drawing is a way into something that is not part of who they are, not part of blowing on your tea or smearing marmalade on bread or combing your hair. The drawings are made from something else that also has been made. The teacher's voice is not in them. Sometimes that voice is reassuring; she almost coos.

But the drawings don't need anyone to coo to them. And you can try to make them accurate, a thrilling notion, a challenge. You can labor intently, lost to everyone around you, until the teacher says it's time to stop. And you can do them on your own, outside of school. You can sit at a table and when your father says, "What's that yer doin'?" you can reply, "Nothin'. Just drawin'." Your father can snort with pleasure or derision, indifference or absent-minded kindliness. You know every nuance of his voice. It doesn't matter, though, because you still have the paper and pencil.

People keep dancing to what they danced to during the war—the big bands. The dancers doodle and canoodle, sway and bounce and swoon until a ballad comes along and they slow dance lovey-dovey-style, two bodies erect but whisper-close. The bodies vibrate with instinct, but the songs peddle a rhyming kingdom that hovers over every dancer's dreamy head. The singers croon, mannerly, smoothing out each wrinkle of emotion. Even when the songs are peppy, the horns hopping, they're still mannerly, crossing their *t*'s, like the penmanship that the children are taught, staying within the lines on the paper, not rising in rampant confusion nor slanting off the page like a name that has lost its last letters. Feelings can be companionable yet suave and airy. The bands are the best of musical worlds and George Harrison's mum and dad know them, know that ballroom where everyone lives in the same fantasy and moves to the same rhythm, where hearts and feet synchronize, where romance's metronome keeps perfect time.

Sound has its own reality. And the joining of hands, the gliding together across the parquet floor, there's something perfect there, something unspoken, something beyond a person's recollections and fears. The words agree: "no more heartaches, no more tears."

Who could argue with that? The words float like a vast draft of kind feeling and soft remorse. The words put grief to bed. The words glimmer with a poetry that life lacks. The words make up for the blank light of Monday morning, the brown despair of habit.

Most people got along with the Americans who came during the war. Many women went to bed with them; more than a few married them. Others didn't care for them—loud, loutish, always calling attention to themselves, braggarts, overbearing extroverts. The British accounts of their drinking bouts and the tall tales they habitually spun began with an amused wink and ended with a grimace. *Yanks*, the tight, rude word described them too well; people in a hurry, rarely gentlemen, or, for that matter, gentlewomen. They'd lifted off the coffin lid of Europe two centuries ago and didn't care what anyone thought. At ease with the improbable, they had room in their vast jumble of geography to range. When they walked down a street, crowded or empty, you felt that. They weren't afraid. Whatever you thought about them, they weren't afraid. Maybe they didn't know any better, maybe they were nothing more than the slangy confidence of their democratic candor, but they walked as if they owned the earth beneath them.

What their bearing had to do with dear old England was questionable. The more educated US soldiers tried to make sense of D.O.E.—Lords and Commons, C of E, dissenters, public schools that were private schools, class boundaries that were invisible yet knife-sharp. Even amid the camaraderie of war there could be snobbery, that mix of manners and contempt, a withering tic that hung on despite the ideological blows of modern times. The war was for freedom and democracy. England was free and democratic but it wasn't America. England was small. It had that lid.

You sit in school and you listen but the teacher isn't talking to you. She's talking all at once to thirty or so children. You understand that this is necessary, that's how schools work, but it doesn't please you. The other children seem to nod along but you want to talk to the teacher on your own. You have lots of questions about why things are the way they are. When you do ask a question, a simple question like "Why do we have to practice writing our names? We know our names already," the teacher says, "Don't be cheeky, Harrison." But you're not being cheeky, or only a little. You're bored.

Sitting there in your wooden chair and being bored isn't the worst thing. You have friends who lost their fathers in the war. You've heard the names of far-off places—El-Alamein, Tobruk, Singapore. You see people with one leg who go about on crutches. You've heard stories about children going over to a friend's house and coming back to no house and no parents. You're lucky, your parents tell you, and you're willing to believe it. When you sit there in the stuffy classroom while someone draws a sleeve across the snot coming out of his nose and someone else yawns and someone else makes a face whenever the teacher turns her back, you can daydream. You're an Arctic explorer, a lion tamer, a mountain climber. And for that amount of time you are. Most of childhood is imagination running in place. When it's something other than imagination, when you intuit something about someone, like your teacher isn't happy or the woman across the street is stuck-up, it's dismissed by adults as childish. Since you're a child, what an adult says has to be true. But it's not fair. That rankles you.

———

In the sultry night a guitar cries out. A black man seated on a wooden bench of sorts, more a plank held up by two rounds of wood, plays it. "Plays," is an approximate word, one of those convenience words. It's more like he is meditating, which is not a word he would use nor would anyone else he knows. Around him the crickets make their intense little racket. They're as much family to him as anything or anyone. They dilute the loneliness that is bound to creep up on him.

He's not singing. The lyrics about two-timing women and back-door men are okay. He likes them for their sly knowledge but the guitar does the real talking. Any string or wire stretched between two pegs or poles can do it. To have these many strings, that's something special to someone rooted in deprivation. It still amazes him.

For slow hours, he's lost to the world of time. He savors some nub of notes, stretches them till it seems they will break, sighs now and then, feeling how much can live in a few bars. The guitar is stolen or "borrowed," as the player likes to put it. He figures that everything is his—guitars, music, women, liquor. The funny thing is that people agree with him, though when it's their woman the men do get touchy. People, his people, put down whatever money they have to hear him play. It eases their pain but does more than that. It makes them happy—get-up-and-shake happy. It makes them forget. It puts them so into their skins that they get out of them. And when he's mournful, they know what he's talking about. Sadness is the sky they were born under.

The guitar man has no complaints about this thick Southern night. It's where he hails from. It will be where he dies. He knows certain roads the way he knows the frayed crazy-quilt that covered the bed he slept in as a child with his two brothers. His uncle gave him his first guitar because he kept bothering the man about it, kept picking it up and strumming every chance he got. His uncle laughed but he listened, too. He nodded and listened more.

No need for anyone to have a name. It's enough that there is the guitar. Names get in the way. Names are for white folks and their police. The guitar man eases into a tune he's known forever. It's a moan, though, more than a tune, music that wobbles and exults at the same time. He can feel the darkness in it. He can feel the caress of it too, how it makes women lie down and spread their legs. It's a sound that comes from the bottom of the world, from the ocean and the earth. It's a sound that disappears in the night but doesn't. The strings have their own life. He knows that he's part of something much bigger than his callused fingers. There is a place called Africa. It's where the sun comes from every day.

The thought comforts him. He's got no home or much cash in his pocket. What he's got is this borrowed guitar. Someone can take that away from him. It's happened before. Some law can take it and whip his black ass. Some law can break it in half and hand it back with a frosty smile. "Here you go, boy. Play that." There's another guitar out there, though. And if there isn't, if this time is the time that ends his time that's all right. He's not looking for favors. The guitar he cradles now like a baby has already given him a big favor. The night is listening to him and nothing beats the night.

It rained a lot in Liverpool, gray weather coming off the water. Inside the flats and houses it rained platitudes, all running together in a predictable skein: *When I was your age I didn't have it so easy I wouldn't mind a bit more I told him you need to get a grip I told him I said I told her.* The people who were speaking were modest people, good folk who did their jobs and complained the way that good folk complain, gently, a bit whiny, once in a long while aggravated, but going along, putting up because *what were you going to do? That's the way life is.* It seemed to George that he could feel the words falling on him, making little dents in him. He could feel the words becoming a second skin. He could feel himself slowing down with all those words in his way. He didn't like to slow down. He had no idea where he was going because people who came from where he came from didn't have ideas like that. People did as they were told. He could see in many people's eyes a furtive misery that came from too much agreeing.

If the words hung onto you and dragged you into something that seemed like living but wasn't, that was boring the way school was boring, someone going on about something you didn't give a crap about and acting as though the world depended on it, that was too bad, that *was your lot and you'd better accept it.* If you raised your hand and said something besides the answer, the teacher nodded, but no one really cared what you thought. Thinking was beside the point. The point was that your thoughtless body filled a seat.

But as he sat at his desk drawing guitars on a sheet of lined paper, he was thinking. And when he heard Elvis, when he heard "Heartbreak Hotel," the voice on the record sounding like nothing he'd ever heard, raw but full, when he heard that unashamed urgent sexy voice that made the singers his parents listened to sound like toy men, when he heard that voice like petrol and honey, a slow sweet beseeching fire, something being said there that never could be taken back no matter how much teachers, parents, and ministers lamented the demise of everything, he knew there was something worth knowing way beyond what everyone near him claimed they knew. That voice didn't care what anyone knew. That voice knew even more than the war knew.

One afternoon he listened to Elvis with a girl. George and the girl, her name was Mary, sat together on a bony, chintz-covered couch in the front room of her brick house that was like a thousand such remaining houses in Liverpool, staunch and cheerless. Some thin, white, almost translucent fabric covered the front windows, indicating that manners and propriety were being attended to. Liverpool was still a city of curtains. Somewhere on the floor above, the girl's mother was, "lying down," according to her daughter who smiled secretively. After a few songs, tunes like "Don't Be Cruel" and "Love Me Tender" and faster ones like "Blue Suede Shoes," George, who had been listening carefully the way he always listened carefully, noting the chords—A, A7—because he was a musician and practiced the guitar till his fingers were raw, looked at Mary, which wasn't hard since she was no more than a foot away. Her face had a glassy expression on it like on a statue of a saint he'd seen once in a church, a real church because he wasn't another straight-through Prot; his mother was Catholic. Mary seemed to be glowing, shaking, and melting at the same time, as if she'd fallen into a furnace of feeling. She'd been telling him before the music started about planning to leave Liverpool and move to Alberta in Canada. Now she wasn't going anywhere. The Tupelo Meteor had hit her.

He wasn't afraid to touch her but she touched first. It wasn't touching, though. It was more like clutching him, grabbing onto him, as if she were drowning. And when she put her face up to his, her kiss wasn't soft and yielding but desperate and fierce. He'd kissed a few girls and gone further than that, but this kiss drilled into him. He felt that he was falling backwards. He wondered if the two of them were going to suffocate because she didn't let up; she kept pressing her lips to his. It seemed, he thought, a good way to die.

After many moments she fell back, her eyes roaming around in her head. She tried to smile but couldn't. Instead, she heaved breathlessly. She started to sob then she convulsed. Her head struck against him, a dull thwack.

"Your mum," he said.

She pulled away and gave him a wide-eyed look. "Damn my mum. Damn everything." Lady-like, she sniffled. "Is that what you're going to do? Be Elvis."

"Be Elvis? He's American. And he's older."

"Don't be thick, George."

He laughed. "How about another kiss?"

Mary wiped at her cheeks with the back of a hand then placed her face an inch or so from George's. "You kiss me this time. You be Elvis."

The world had to go somewhere. Europe not only had spent itself; it had turned Death into a spendthrift. "Look," said Death, "millions. I'm rich." Expositions, buildings, machines, speeches: Europe's splendid progress made for a wretched mockery. In the face of the material train moving ever forward, Evil had answered back. Evil took a much longer view. Evil knew that well-meaning people were at a loss about how to stand up. Many people didn't believe in evil. They had much more sophisticated designations. Imagine how Evil chortled when the phrase "dialectical materialism" presented itself. Or people didn't want to die to oppose evil. Who could throw the first stone at Neville Chamberlain? Many Czechs could, but British people shook their heads when his name came up, the shaking being a code for the most mixed feelings. Neville had wanted to be a good man but he was a weak man.

Force could battle evil but never answer it. Only spirit could do that. When the saint faced whatever thug was ruling whatever satrapy in whatever century, the saint never argued. The saint spoke for spirit's invisible spark, the connection of conscience to divinity. In the course of the two world wars, saints—a few recognized but many more obscured—stood up and died. After the war, every minute of teaching should have gone into recounting their lives. All those children sitting at their desks in Nantes, Liverpool, Rotterdam, Dresden, Hamburg, Moscow needed to learn about such people . . . but who wanted to linger there? Saints were for extremities. Europe had been to that ghastly show. Weren't they called "theaters of war"?

Rory Storm and the Hurricanes, the band Ringo was in, wore coats and ties. That was show business. You see pictures of George and the other lads with ties and coats, too, but you have the feeling that something is going on in their bright eyes that doesn't have to do with show business. You get the feeling that something is happening beyond the agreeable, money-making pretenses of *we'll play and you applaud and we'll all go home and forget it tomorrow.* George had nothing against the money that could buy the cars and motorbikes he liked. The pretending bothered him, though. Music wasn't an act.

Yes, you showed up and put on a show. He played in places that were little more than dens and caves. In Germany he would play in bars where people were so drunk they didn't even know a band was on the stage. The music, though, had to be real. The music couldn't be the prattle his parents had gone in for. They needed such music, the horns just jumpy enough to be alive but smooth, too, always smooth. Melody like warm jam.

What was real was more than an adolescent question, more than confusion shading into instinctive rebellion. It concerned a large human matter in denatured modern times: How were we to know we were alive? When George left for Hamburg, he was "just seventeen," but youth worked for him, not against him. He had a way of being open while also standing a bit to the side, an amused bystander. He seemed to understand that more was going on than he ever was going to take in. He was fine with that. The point was to be alert and not be looking over your shoulder. He would never have said that the Beatles' songs at the beginning were deep. If they invited ridicule from more educated ears, that was those ears' problem. Wanting to hold a girl's hand or learning that a girl still loved you were as valid feelings as any. What some journalists purveyed as shrill and hopelessly simple was also startlingly alive.

When George played those importuning songs, he wasn't purveying any notion of anything. He was there in the song. It was heartfelt, catchy, and something like delirious. You could say he was a kid who didn't know any better but you could also say that his taut yet weltering sound was homespun genius. He had nothing to lose. What he had on his mind and in his growing soul were the Americans who, of necessity, were making it up. Elvis and Chuck Berry and Little Richard and Carl Perkins seemed to truly come from nowhere. One minute there was no such music and then there was.

When George hefted his guitar something in the air prepared to move. Outside the Cavern Club, the long queue, a dark overcoated teenage throng waiting patiently to indulge ecstasy, knew that. From the sleep of after-the-war these youths (a word the newspapers favored) had emerged only recently into the dank light of day. They knew what they liked and weren't shy about proclaiming it. When the girls started screaming, it was like Elvis or even Sinatra, but it was happening right there in Liverpool. It was crazy, out of control, primal, pulling your hair and wailing and weeping like some ancient Greek rite when people didn't believe in one god offering salvation. It was about the music and sex but the screaming was deeper and stranger. It was about being moved in a place that had not been moved before, a Bermuda Triangle of flesh, heart, and mind. It was about feelings coming out that had not been mapped before. Seized by frenzied joy—wouldn't you scream too?

Amid the colossal dullness of getting along, of pretending to care, there appeared these satyrs with guitars.

"George!" some girls are screaming. "George!" He smiles back but he's serious. The girls know that. They scream even louder for his being serious. He isn't some cute airhead. He's got that look that says, "I know something you may not know." He's confident and a little cocky. They scream even louder. It seems impossible they could scream so loud. They must have amplifiers inside them. When they scream George's name, it's a plea, an invocation, a yearning, and a ravished call. George nods. What's surprising is that he's not surprised. He knows there is wildness out there and in himself, which amuses and excites him or, once in a long while, saddens him. He has a feeling for life's margins. Hamburg taught him that but it's more his instincts. When he starts writing his own songs, they speak to the margins, the oddments, the buried emotions, the hovering spirits.

Love—why would you want to get away from it? Why didn't the world devote itself to love? What was wrong with love? And not just the erotic fuse of young people getting humpy, but love that leapt over smugness and grief, love that saw through every human dodge, love that was loving. He thought about that. He was happy singing the songs but sensed the songs were only the bottom rung of a tall ladder. The Cavern Club wasn't an ultimate place, just the way Liverpool wasn't an ultimate place. Nothing against either one but there was more to love than the proverbial Lovely Girl.

Once he and the others had passed through that byway, enjoying every sensual turn in an elaborate yet basic road, something vast opened up. You could give it any fancy name—art, meditation, higher love—but it was real and felt attainable because no one had gone down this particular road before. Blokes had written books and directed movies and made music but they hadn't been worldwide sensations. They hadn't filled up stadiums. The joke for George was that the success was about other people's notions. The success was like being in school and listening about How the World Was. You worked hard; you got a lucky break or two; you made it to the top; you smiled for the cameras. He could do that, but it was like being in a silly play. No one knew who he was. No one knew what he thought. Even when a microphone was in his face, he was first and foremost a Beatle.

Being a Beatle was happenstance. What the world considered permanent—the Beatles' John-Paul-George-Ringo solidity—wasn't permanent at all. Standing in a hotel window and looking at the crowds below, he thought about how absurd all this was. No matter how many records were sold, they were a passing fancy. He turned his back to the window and looked at those in the room with him. Just being alive was a passing fancy.

That feeling didn't make him grim. There was nothing grim about those throbbing girls. It was crazy but it was a craziness any guy would envy. There were no proportions, however. When he'd drawn those Gothic details back in school, everything had to be in proportion. Life had its proportions—stay up all night and you'd yawn in the morning. History didn't have proportions, though. Those people in Liverpool didn't deserve those bombs. Things could get terribly out of hand.

He was born into a world where little was expected of him beyond doing as he was told. Though such a life seemed real—going off to a job and coming home to a wife and kids and the patter on the television and a bit of fun on the weekends, it never encountered anything beyond its agreed-upon confines. There was no music to it. One reason he and his bandmates loved to mock the various authorities' sure-footed answers was that no one knew where music came from or why there was such a thing. What mattered—and he felt this in his very hands—was that music spoke in a way nothing else spoke. Music made him free in a way that few people managed to be free. If that was mystical, then it was mystical. The interviewers who tried to pin him down with their questions about "Eastern religion" or "cults" or "LSD" were looking for a shortcut but there was none.

He could be someone who could find out who was observing him in the mirror. Yes, he was George: a substantial portion of the world knew his name but recognition wasn't a compliment. It meant you had become a billboard. It could happen to anyone. What he wondered about was becoming someone without a function, someone who could play when he wanted to play and go where he wanted to go, someone on the other side of the billboard. Everyone talked about liberation, but the vision of being more than a captive was stunning. Even Elvis had been a captive. What George intuited was that each life was music. We were here for a while, like a tune, some longer and some shorter, and then we were gone. Our beauty lay in the intensity of our passing. Music celebrated that force with its own force.

You could wink at that tuneful quality. Like those shrieking girls, you could revel in it. You could walk away in favor of more serious matters but the music remained. George raised his dark eyebrows and mugged for the photographers but he kept his eye on the magical notes. "Stop daydreaming, Harrison," more than one teacher had said to him. "No," he had replied.

MILES DAVIS

THE ALPHA AND OMEGA OF THE LOWDOWN, the don't-push-me-around, the downtown, midtown, and uptown was: What would Miles say?

The trouble with fays—there was a lot of trouble with fays but the primary trouble—was that they didn't believe. It was true that anyone whose head was attached to his or her neck was going to say, "Hold on, every cracker believes in Jesus," and that person was right. But that was what the trouble was. The fays were selfish. They wanted to hold on to everything for themselves. So even when they were busy believing, they were looking over their shoulders and worrying whether the niggers' believing messed up their believing. They wanted to keep Jesus in their pocket. They didn't really believe in fishes and loaves because if you believed that, then you believed in sharing—not preaching but sharing, inviting niggers into your house as if they weren't niggers! And the natural stuff they should have believed in, like spirits, ghosts, gypsy women, crossroads, the hocus-pocus from the red clay American earth, they winked at. They made a little smile as if someone pinched them, as if Jesus cast that heathen shit out and left it for minstrel jokes about darkies walking through the graveyard.

The educated fays were worse, though. "We're reasonable people," they said. Whenever you heard that, you had better watch out. The crackers scratched and sniffed and lurched in some mean circles but the educated fays moved straight ahead. "Reason, get in here and clean this mess up." Reason was the whitest. There was no lightning in reason's sky. You fall out of love, rich people toss themselves out of tall buildings, revolutions kill millions, and reason comes in, clears his throat (because reason is a man, got to be a man) and gives an explanation.

Reason had race reasons, too: "The reason the Negro is an inferior being … Scientists who have measured the Negro skull … The mental capacity of the Negro has been determined to be …" Reason took prejudice's hand and went for a walk in the segregated park. Reason soothed the fays listening to lectures by so-called experts, the way Jesus soothed the crackers. Jesus soothed the niggers, too, but it was different—the niggers had been in the true storm. They knew the wind and rain weren't fooling. They could smell Jesus's blood like the crucifixion was yesterday.

Long ago, the fays had won the game because they had made up the rules. They owned 'most every inch. They could laugh while despising you. What more could they want? Maybe their nastiness was because they couldn't own bodies the way they used to. Or maybe it was as simple as death; that they had a grudge against death, how death takes away everybody's name, no matter how big and white you are. Selfish and childish, the fays sucked the marrow out of the bone and then complained.

When Miles Davis said "motherfucker" every third word, that was a protest—not like waving a sign or lying down on the sidewalk or marching, but still a protest against the game of goodness the fays played: "If you would just be good Negroes, everything would be fine." But for most fays a good Negro was a contradiction in terms. It was adding value to something worthless.

Miles knew that. You would have to be a very unusual Negro not to know that. Miles knew the cloud of denigration and derision, spoken and unspoken—all the racial crud—that circled his brilliant, seething head. How could it not bug him? It had destroyed better men than he. When he got brusque, that was temperament but there was something metaphysical, too. "Motherfucker" was a state of being—armor and attack, playful and dismissive. A man had to be ready. Harsh shit was harsh shit.

You might want to say, "That's where the music came in," but the music didn't come in through any finger-popping door. The music was the unchanging setting, the complete dramatic works, the tail and the dog, genesis and apocalypse. The music wasn't bequeathed because not much was bequeathed. Much more was begrudged than bequeathed. You could argue that the only inviolable was the invisible soul but the fays tried to take that, too.

The music was earned but there was nothing heavy about it. Even the funeral marches weren't heavy but were light on death's feet, droning away at eternity. The music was like the boxers Miles favored—also light on their feet yet possessed of knock-out power. And like the best boxers in the ring, the music wasn't predictable, couldn't be pinned down or planned ahead of time. The boxers had their combinations of punches and the musicians had their chords but how those got put together depended on the genius of the moment.

The anecdotes about people trying to control the music and take credit for the music when the credit wasn't theirs, especially fays, and how Miles felt about that, were endless. It wasn't a new situation. Fays blacked up in the last century, at once ridiculing and stealing Negro identity. When Miles used to add "and that shit" to almost any sentence, it often felt like a reference to that weary history. "And that shit" was the baggage he and his brethren carried. If he kept looking over his shoulder, it was understandable. There may not have been a hellhound on his trail, but lots of fays were ready to claim what wasn't theirs.

Playing out there on the race line could make a warm person cold. Miles could be hell iced over. Some star-struck kid would come up for an autograph, something harmless, and Miles would start swearing like the guy had murdered Miles's grandmother. Or he was terse, the weight of all that bad shit of history in a few cutting words. Or he didn't say anything because what was there to say? What was there to say to Chet Baker being picked ahead of Miles in the jazz magazine polls? It wasn't like Chet didn't understand what was going down. Those polls of the "critics" weren't his fault. Musicians took from one another because that was what musicians did. What was embarrassing was when the tributary got chosen over the source. Miles never said that Chet didn't have music in his white soul. The music was indifferent to color. And Chet, beginning but not ending with drug addiction, had his own problems.

You could say heroin was one more case of fays aping Negro hipness and that may have been true. The grief ran deeper than that, though, much deeper. Heroin was a personal map to nowhere that destroyed every metaphor, knocking out the human essence and leaving a person more like a nonperson—"nodding."

Why a jazzman would need that shit—to use the word that denominated the drug—would be a fair question. There was no shortage of good times: the excitement, at times bliss, of the music, of meeting other musicians and finding common ground, to say nothing of the women who hung around and weren't shy about their charms. Yet behind the boozy conviviality, camaraderie, and sex, behind the thrill of discovery that seemed encoded in the music, there remained an ache—a dark, collective voice in a darker night. One place memory went was the music—and the memories could be brutal. Inside the articulate trumpet of Miles Davis was an inarticulate cry.

The bebop guys were like a platoon that had gone ahead of the rest of the army and didn't have any lines of supply. Out there on their own, they had one another but little else. Innovation wasn't a big pedestal to stand on, especially when a lot of people didn't like the innovation, didn't like the riffs, tempos, and sheer strangeness of bebop. The jazz of the big bands that kept Americans dancing through World War II had been peppy, practiced yet tinged with the romantic. As a suave skein of concerted sound, the music seemed a form of social perfection. The beboppers could play that shit (as Miles would say) but didn't care to. They preferred to investigate the moments within the skein. They preferred music that was inward yet visceral, not danceable in a swing-and-sway way but listenable in a darkened-small-nightclub way where people sat at little tables and took in enormities of elastic yet taut feeling. Bop was assertive but speculative, an unpredictable punch in the musical gut. In the moments were angles, silences, tumbles, intuitive leaps followed by more intuitive leaps. Bop—that percussive, stark word—startled more than it soothed. When some musicians heard the prodigious Charlie Parker, they thought *this is impossible*. But his music was an impossibility made real. His music was a dare that had been taken up and made good on. You could walk away but you couldn't deny it. There were all those white guys in history books in their funny clothes—explorers—and then there were these black guys who were explorers, too.

The music didn't fit into the nation at large with its marching bands and cowboy songs and hit parade, its how much was that doggie in the window. It didn't fit into any scheme of education. Miles's year at Juilliard might have been an allegory of the chasm between the European tradition and what was happening at one in the morning at Minton's Playhouse on 118th Street. The music didn't fit into any professional scheme of what a person was supposed to do with his life. What it literally did fit into were the tiny stages where a musician had to take care to not fall off. People went to the jazz clubs to hang out and listen closely or not closely but then they went home and got up in the morning and did whatever they did to make their livings. For the jazz guys, though, the clubs were their livings and that was a very different life. Like islands, the clubs were their own worlds, cozy if cramped, but vulnerable to fashion pressures, money pressures, politics, graft, and the police. As the NYC cabaret card issued to each performer testified, playing in the clubs was revocable. Bad people—dope users—could be punished and were punished. Playing jazz was a privilege not a right. No one was above the law—a piety invoked when some cop or councilman hadn't been paid off. Genius was irrelevant.

"Well, motherfucker, if genius isn't relevant, then what is?" Miles could have told anyone who wanted to hear, which would have been more or less no one.

When Miles hung out with Jean-Paul Sartre in Paris, he said they talked, which was like saying you spent time with the Pope and you prayed. Who knows what either side of that conversation sounded like, but one aspect had to be the dodgy manner of being found in the word *improvisation*. You can imagine Miles checking out Sartre about that word and maybe Sartre, a square but a French square, getting it, getting the existential quality of the word, the quality that cut loose from the ponderousness of what was supposed to be, of the dubious expectations, instead trusting the contingent nature of the fingers on the horn and the lips on the mouthpiece. *Embouchure* was a French word, after all.

It was after Paris, after Sartre and Juliette Greco, a woman who took Miles's standard encomium "fine bitch" to a whole other level, that Miles fell into heroin. *Being and Nothingness* was a book title Miles would have understood, not in any highfalutin way but as a summary of what was going down each day. The music pierced the nothingness, enlivened it, but despite the making of records, music was inherently transitory. The *being* part of the equation hung over Miles's head and lots of other heads and wouldn't go away. In the outer world the music had nowhere to turn; all it could do was tunnel ever more deeply into the musicians' inner worlds. That may sound curious, as if the music wasn't created by the musicians but, as any of them would have told you, the music had its own life. That led to sheer magic at more times than ever would be counted, times when the musicians not only heard one another but heard the possibility that was in the next bar or chord or phrase and jumped into it with alacrity and intelligence. It also led to depression, confusion, and sheer dread. The beboppers were communicating the incommunicable; a sense of life based on creating music from purloined, discarded, and—yes, there was the word—improvised instruments. Puffing away contentedly on his pipe and ever talking, now certain and now skeptical, Sartre epitomized someone from the land of Descartes. There was more than an ocean between France and the jazzmen's land of the blue notes. The sweet sting of being in those notes offered an eloquence that toppled mere thought.

Such eloquence didn't come easy and Miles didn't lack for self-destructive examples. He played months and months of nights beside Charlie Parker and watched close-up one of the virtuoso performances in the annals of fucking up. Miles liked to say that genius was greedy and that Bird was the greediest motherfucker there was. If the beboppers formed a battalion, then Bird was the chief scout. He was one irregular scout, though, someone who not only made up the music but made up his life, too. Plenty of people, particularly in America, did that, but Bird had no script to go by. His nickname epitomized his being, a big man trying to fly. When he played he flew. When he didn't play, he still flew but he flew like a chicken with its head chopped off. He flew desperate and blind. He couldn't bury himself fast enough.

Running amok made a certain sense because in America it seemed that was what artists had to do to be artists. No one much understood or cared. The business of America was business; the marketplace dictated all values; success meant money; heroes were businessmen and ballplayers. Everyone knew that litany and everyone had to live with it. The indifference and contempt shown to artists were genial in the good-natured American way—no hard feelings, mister, but you can drop dead for all I care. And it wasn't as though Miles had set out to be an artist. He was a musician. He made music in clubs where people drank, danced, flirted, kissed, got into arguments, passed out, etc., not in some symphony hall where Mrs. Millionaire showed off her diamonds and cultural pretensions. Miles knew the smells of too many bodies in too small a space. You might be an artist avowing the power of your imagination but you had to have a strong stomach, too.

Watching Bird—as true an artist as ever existed—was like watching a ship go down. The foundering took years but was relentless and Miles felt that. What was worse was when his own ship started to go down, when he started stealing, lying, and looking like a pile of rags—he who was as sharp a dresser as anyone—because of dope. In America you're supposed to pull yourself up with your own strength but that was another fay myth to justify who had the power and who didn't, like saying some sharecropping Negro in Alabama could grow up and become president. Miles knew that shit. He knew how fays wanted to be thanked for doing nothing. And he knew how Bird's suffering went hand in hand with Bird's powerlessness. It took two hells to tango.

It wasn't emulation of suffering, which he mocked, nor was it self-pity that led Miles down Bird's sorry path—he didn't have any of that in him. Even when he was pimping and thinking of nothing more than his next score, he scoured himself morally. That was how he was brought up and that wasn't going away. Being confident but uneasy, contemptuous of anyone who didn't measure up but bleeding self-contempt—look at what he'd done to himself—he went after his sorry psyche like the mental boxer he was. "You're a worthless motherfucker. You're a musician who's never going to let the fay world put you in a box." Left-right, left-right, left-right. Someone was going to win someday—if he survived.

While the decision hung in the balance, the music kept growing. There were enough people making the music so the sound jumped from club to club, hall to hall, city to city, coast to coast. Despite all the bad shit around the music—hangers-on, promoters who promoted themselves first of all, fay critics who didn't know squat and didn't care to know squat—the music kept moving. This might seem to be the progress mania that America was always touting—newer, bigger, better—but jazz wasn't like that. Jazz was roots and respect. When Miles got pissed at some of the guys who went off and played "free," he was thinking "free of what? What you want to be free for? Wasn't there endless room already?" Like Monk, hadn't he devoted himself to finding the space not just between the notes but above, below, and behind them? Wasn't he exploring sheer being?

But it wasn't only freedom that drove the free players. There was anger that a million incidents had called forth. You could be going about your business and living your life, but a black man was never just living his life. Targets don't live lives the way others live lives. When a New York detective cracked Miles on the head in front of the club where he was playing, the blow was as much shaming and infuriating as physically hurtful. He was high-strung, impetuous, not going to take shit from anybody, but the anger that came from being attacked in public for being a black man who had just ushered a white woman into a cab and was told to "move on" went further. That anger became a fact, another dark, personal sun in the world-that-white-folks-made. That was where journalists and second-hand people in general criticized Miles even more. He was said to be testy. He was full of no good shit. He wasn't a grateful American. He didn't truckle. Worst of all, he was bitter. No one in America could be bitter.

It was unforgivable. That was how simple some people could be. But they hadn't had their head cracked open on a sidewalk in New York. They hadn't seen their own blood flowing. They hadn't been told they were troublemakers, disturbers of the peace, and, of course, niggers.

Over and over, the sum of his talented days came back to "motherfucker." It was almost comical how you could play things no one could imagine and give people feelings that made them deeper, stronger, and truer, give them music every bit as important as Bach and Beethoven and whoever else Juilliard threw at the nineteen-year-old from East Saint Louis, but it came back to "motherfucker." It came back to someone muttering the word or sobbing the word or screaming the word. It came to someone standing on a street corner at night and wondering how to get home when there was no home. It came to Miles throwing any shit he could get his hands on at his wife, hitting her and knowing what a sorry-ass man he was to do that. Contempt was a two-way street. It would have been nice to be civilized, to live civilized, to be recognized as civilized, but that wasn't the way it went down. The vise held him as tightly as it held anyone—maybe more.

Bands broke up. Guys died. Guys moved on. Guys said, "Fuck it, all these kids want is shake their fay asses to rock and roll." Guys went off with chicks. Guys kept doing drugs. Guys gave up.

There never was any *supposed to be.* How could there be? It was only sound, to begin with. Light, heavy, thick, round—the adjectives Miles used were real but unreal, too. When people said they didn't like the music or they didn't understand the music, they meant that the music wasn't comfortable to them. That was fair. Even when seductively beautiful, the music was never meant to lull or simply insinuate itself. It pushed against melody continual-ly. Harmonies were found where they didn't seem to exist. The search for a new way to disassemble and then reassemble the tune was constant. Why not leave things the way they were? Why spend your life going out on limbs?

Those weren't Miles Davis sorts of questions. "Miles born with a tack in his ass," more than one musician was prone to say about him, and because they knew him the sentence was al-most kindly, almost gentle. Miles wasn't trying to be difficult; he was difficult. "What the hell's wrong with that?" you can imag-ine him saying. "You want Glenn Miller or Benny Goodman, go listen to Glenn Miller or Benny Goodman." Miles was modern: he honored the self-aware spirit of Time. Time, as in keeping time in the band, that second-by-second aliveness of listening and acting, and Time as wayward god, were all he had, which were more than enough, because Miles saw how dreary and use-less clock-time was, how the permeable moment held everything there was to hold. He got that when he heard Bird play, how time could jounce and wallow at the same time, how Bird was an instinctive modernist, a time fucker. However pissed Miles was with the state of everything, he delighted, throughout his career, in breaking time down and, inventor-like, finding what was there.

For all his acting as though things were cool, Miles Davis wasn't comfortable with much. The edge he carried around nev-er let up because the world's edge—racial and otherwise—didn't let up either. And for all the bravado, he understood the place of compassion. He wasn't the only sufferer. How else could he get along with the likes of the sensitive souls—Coltrane, Bill Evans, the drummer Art Taylor—he dealt with? Throughout his life he was always putting together bands and a true band was a group of people who played together because they felt something for one another that was in the music but beyond the music, too. His great bands were the joint ventures of rampant individualists.

It wasn't that the world could eat up a nigger/Negro/Afro American/black. No matter the nominating, visible tag (to say nothing of being invisible), the world that was America did that routinely, but Miles refused that fate. Or he was, first of all, hell on himself so he beat the world to the punch. The music fit him so well because it resisted all shrines, all memorializing, all homilies. The fays built shrines to a lot skinnier shit than jazz improvisation, but as he stood on the bandstand of this or that club in this or that American city, he could live in the possibilities of the tunes and the dynamics of the players he'd assembled. Despite the separating finesse of the endeavor, the you-have-to-find-your-voice-not-someone-else's, jazz was as socialized as any ritual music played by any tribe on the planet. Out of the lonesomeness of hearing what was in your head and approaching it boldly and warily, came solidarity—and a lot of flat-out, soul-expanding good times.

The good times were not only the high of the music, the going to places where you didn't think you could go and the feeling of being radically *present* that was the best of all feelings, but the carrying on, the over and over impact of connecting. That achievement was bittersweet: Miles saw how Bird died and how Billie died. Their deaths were ugly and wrong. The grief of how they left this world, the pathos that was so much less than who they were, assailed him, but it was grief he had to accept if he was going to keep making music because whether the people who sat there in front of the band had too much or too little, they all were caught up in the sad identifying shit that went with wearing a suit or a dress, a name and an address, to say nothing of their skin color. They needed some music to show them they were human, not some toe-tapping jive but music that went into their hearts and heads at the same time, music that woke them the existential fuck up.

There weren't many questions that Miles didn't get asked. Coltrane called him "the teacher." He was the first one to be interviewed for *Playboy*. It made sense, because Miles knew more than anyone. He hadn't just persevered. He had seized the storm and made it his own. Not only was he not afraid of it, he reveled in it.

The questions were never easy. They were bound to be impertinent because they sought to melt the unsayable, the musical, into the verbal and worse, because so many interviewers were possessed of a perverse hunger to unmask the party they were interviewing, to get at something no one yet had gotten at, to make Miles Davis sound glib or forlorn or merely cynical. There was that bad feeling in the modern world that a person didn't exist until he or she had been serially interviewed, until fame had been wrung out like a washcloth.

The answers to the musical questions were always arresting—what he looked for in a drummer, how he handled the mute. But the bigger questions hovered over a pit that held snakes. Even if an innovator such as Miles was greeted with open arms, the response was still bound to be largely uncomprehending. No one else could be as inside the music as he was. No one could know the thousand emotional nodes that caused the music. No one could know how the music was unbidden and dedicated. No one could know the quirks and impulses and longings and certainties and probing and downright ecstasy. What was there to *say* about that? How could words be anything more than filigree? How could questions and answers not create a false certainty and repose? How could they not make people feel that the musician-artist who answered them was more solid than he really was?

"Shit, man."

So, as almost invariably happened, when some interviewer sought to pull back the curtain of his soul, Miles stood ready to set fire to the curtain. He was on fire already, one of those burners like Kierkegaard or Dostoevsky. The terms of his era were different but he spoke from the same source: "If there was a God, he would be in the cancer wards, in the hospitals—or over in Korea and Vietnam."

When asked what he saw in the future, he used to reply "Tomorrow."

No disrespect, of course. Talking into a tape recorder was another part of getting from day to day. He could live with that, how there was no finality. That was why there was music.

AUDREY HEPBURN

THERE IS A STORY. A princess comes to Rome. She is tired of being a princess, which is so terribly official and so terribly boring, which could turn a vibrant young woman into a mannequin. She escapes from her entourage and falls asleep, much like a princess, near the Coliseum. A journalist finds her there and allows her to spend the night at his place. Soon he recognizes who the woman sleeping in his apartment really is. The next day he and a crony take her around Rome. At last she feels free to gallivant—getting her hair cut, eating ice cream, and racing around on a motor scooter. The princess and the journalist fall in love that day but it is only for a day. They must return to their lives and their obligations. And they do.

There is a story. A woman is about to divorce her husband. She returns to her home in Paris to find it bare, stripped of every possession. Furthermore, her husband is dead. He was tossed off a moving train. Happily or strangely or coincidentally or all the above, the woman has met a man who shows up and says he will help her. Who is this man? He has many names. Meanwhile, the woman learns that her husband filched a fortune and that others believe she has that fortune. They are willing to kill to retrieve that fortune. But she doesn't know where it is. Over and over she protests that she doesn't know where it is. She isn't lying. She seems incapable of lying.

And there is a story. Two filthy-rich brothers live in a mansion on Long Island. They are so rich they have a chauffeur. The chauffeur has a daughter who has recently returned from Paris. Everything important in the world of emotion emanates from Paris, not from Long Island. The young woman is beautiful, scintillating, and full of the most marvelous life. Which brother will end up with her? But more to the point, is she interested in either of them? She has been to Paris. They are used to looking down; now they have to look up.

These are stories that compose the plots of movies, but they are the stuff of fairy tales, too: princesses, fortunes, wishes, and mistaken identities. They could not have happened but on the screen they do. That sense of impossibility coming true is the most delicious fabrication, for above all, movies purvey romance. There must be something heady and swooning and yet difficult that informs falling in love. There must be something magical because love is magical. No one knows where it comes from or how long it will last or whether both people will feel it. Love is the last incalculable. Lust is boorish and sweaty; romance burns with a cool heat. It inspires wit. It fences with feelings. It is a prelude that may somehow become a full-blown, life-long symphony, every day shot through with deep kisses. Or it may fizzle into indifference or contempt or revulsion. The swelling, lyrical strings on the soundtrack only last so long. That, however, is the beauty of movies. They don't have to tell the whole story because no one really wants the whole story. People sit there in the dark to inhabit the part of the story where the princess wakes up or the treasure is found or the brothers weep for love. The whole story is tedious. That's why there are artists—to find the magic part of the story.

There are endless competing stories, like the young girl who hid in an attic and confided her feelings to a diary. Like the princess or the young woman who returned from Paris, she was full of life. It was all wrong that she had to hide but there was no fairy tale within her story. Her story occurred in the bloody, shrieking maw of history. She was fifteen when she died. No one even knew how many were murdered nor could numbers have told what it was like to hold your breath when you heard footsteps on the stairs or wish you could go outside to feel the wind in your hair or be shepherded to your pointless death.

What are people supposed to make of that story? Are they supposed to continue with their daily tasks? Or are they supposed to say, "This must not happen again anywhere?" Or are they supposed to forget, as if that story of the girl with glasses and dark hair never happened? Or are the stories of wars and killings too much for the person who pushes some money forward and announces to the ticket seller, "One, please."

One mere person! When the Hollywood moguls insisted on a happy ending they knew that one life could only support so much bleak weight. They knew that this was another beauty of the movies. They were weightless. They occurred on a screen suspended in darkness in midair. Even when they portrayed the eventual murder of a fifteen-year-old girl, there was something weightless present. The movies were another realm. They organized contrivance in ways that exceeded every known art. They possessed an inherent magic, a blend of machine and spirit no one had imagined before. No one would ever improve on that magic because like a masque or mummery it was unique.

Audrey did not grow up at the movies. She was born in the same year as Anne Frank and she lived during the war in the same country. Their faces show the same delicate, irrepressible vitality.

It was brutally cold. There was no heat. They were rounding up people. There was no more food. You could hear rifle shots. It was the middle of the twentieth century and people were eating grass. They tried to make bread out of grass. The children cried and cried. People got very sick and died. Some people were taken from their homes and executed. Many homes were set fire to. People trudged along on roads, though they didn't know where to go. They had only their lives. They tried to hold on but it felt that there was nothing to hold on to. Every lasting stay had fallen away. Every story had crumpled.

If you have the emptiness of war in your stomach, you might save out a bit of food. Or maybe if you have food, you will gorge until you pass out. Either way the emptiness will have consumed you.

Audrey wanted to dance. There was that letting go and that spirited grace. "This is how the body speaks," one of her teachers said.

The poise came naturally to her. Amid the large and small tragedies—war, and her father leaving when she was a little girl—something in her grasped how precious balance was. The ballet poses emanated from classical attitudes—the joy of rigor—but what underlay those poses was the tenuous arc between the unbearable and the bearable. Great feeling was bound to wobble.

Audrey was too tall to be a ballerina, and the war left her behind those who had continued to study. Still, she could dance. She was filled with springy, boisterous energy and yet, unlike the century she was born into, she didn't believe in the genius of restlessness. For the twentieth century, nothing could be merely harmless, old-fashioned, and even a bit charmed in the way that peasants once considered a tree or a star or a donkey to be charmed. For the twentieth century, there had to be vanguards moving ever forwards and vanguards in front of vanguards. Death to Baba Yaga! Death to Simple Hans! Death to Rapunzel! Death to fairies and sprites and elves! Fancy—the midsummer's night's talent for turning nothing into something—was one of the century's first casualties.

One of the wonders of this mere girl-woman was her ability to stick out her tongue and make a face. If you can't make fun of What Is Important, you can't have fun. Instinctively, children know that—it's part of how they survive—but adults too often prefer the future to the now. They have sworn sacred oaths. They have consecrated tasks. They have class enemies, ethnic enemies, tribal enemies, religious enemies. They have powerful words that can both summon and unleash loathing. A child intuits all this wretched seriousness in adults, their wrenched faces and tight words. In her plucky way, the child mattered much more than the men on podiums haranguing crowds and commanding armies. They can murder her of course, the way they murdered Anne Frank. But though they can try, they can't murder everyone.

One of the wonders of Audrey was her ability to make fun of herself. She could let her ego pass by. Between who she was and who at any given time she might become there was a movable distance that nurtured and settled her. She could play a princess or daughter of a chauffeur with equal ardor. She possessed within her narrow body great latitude. When, in a hotel in Monte Carlo, Colette recognized Audrey as the perfect Gigi for a forthcoming

Broadway version—a total, utterly unpredictable happenstance—it made perfect sense. Audrey was waiting but not waiting. She was simply present. Colette wrote that Audrey was "piquant." More than once Colette had stuck out her sly tongue. She knew what she was looking for.

Audrey protested. She had never acted on the stage. She had been a chorine and bit player in a few not very good movies. Doubt and honesty made a tandem inside of Audrey for a lifetime. Colette, who would not have been a bad choice as a role model for a female deity, reassured her. In her worldly way, Colette understood how the twentieth century needed female deities desperately. "Piquant" was part of the description; so were graceful, resilient, candid, and marvelously vital, a pure spark of the life force.

Sometimes the word "worship" was used to define the adoration a movie star like Audrey could elicit. An embarrassing word but an understandable one, not because the screen was famously larger than life but because the camera showed people in a way people never had been shown. Audrey's face with its delicacy and seeming guilelessness was meant for close-ups. It wasn't that she had extraordinary dramatic range so much as an ability to convey tiny, moment-by-moment shifts in her being. There was no great rage or pity in her. There was, however, a talent for being herself, even as she was being someone else.

A deity can't do that. A deity is stuck, cursed with omnipotence. People can believe or disbelieve but a god—to say nothing of the monotheistic God—is timeless. If modern times were bereft of the greater certainties, the shifts of actors on screens offered an uncanny degree of recompense. Two or so hours of agreeable oblivion did not equal salvation, but Audrey had seen what the Nazis did to prayers.

She was patient as she went through take after take with fussy directors like William Wyler, but she had no patience for male sanctimony. When, as often happened in her movies, a man began to lecture her, you knew she was waiting, beneath a smile or pout, to dish it back to him. She didn't trust in the world that men had made. If, as an actress, no one asked her for an opinion beyond clothes and what-is-Gregory-Peck-really-like, that only showed the poverty of thought that surrounded her. Her pretty head was much more than pretty.

Truman Capote complained that Audrey wasn't the right actress for *Breakfast at Tiffany's*, but Truman Capote liked to complain. It was one way he knew he was alive. Pique was his oxygen. Supposedly, Audrey played a call girl in the story but there was little to no hint of sex in the movie made from Capote's book. Holly Golightly's modus operandi was to duck out to the ladies room after taking fifty bucks from the guy and not come out. It wasn't a great way to spend your life but it didn't seem to particularly matter to her. She lived in her imagination as much as she lived in New York City. The importunate human race was a humdrum bother to her. She was a romantic, which was to say, a person who honored her feelings in a world that didn't honor feelings.

There is nothing especially realistic in how Holly Golightly is portrayed. We don't see pissed-off guys stave in the ladies room door or haggle about the specifics of her services. She is charming and thus adroit at keeping the world at bay. That seems part of Audrey's core. The world will violate you one way or another. What happens after romance is the tedium of getting along with another person. In that sense movies that delved into marriage had to be comedies of the sort the other Hepburn often starred in. One weighty, stupid, confused day must collide with another, yet somehow or other the wires of romance must be reattached.

Holly Golightly is not one for marriage. Her comedy is about isolation, its pleasures and pitfalls. Holly must be saved from that state, no matter that she seemed quite okay staring in Tiffany's windows all by herself and that the love interest was George Peppard, who managed to be both preening and wooden at the same time. The two of them must kiss in the rain at the end of the movie to affirm romance, even though the beauty of Holly is that she doesn't give a rat's ass for the lower forms of romance. It isn't that she is hard; Audrey could never have portrayed someone who was hard. Holly's eye is set on a higher prize.

Tiffany's symbolizes that prize, but a viewer feels that more is going on with Holly and with Audrey than standing outside in the early morning and looking at jewelry. Holly believes in beauty and style, and Audrey as Holly embodies that. The notion of Holly as merely a call girl—someone to fuck—is ludicrous. It isn't that Audrey isn't sexy. In her coy, breathless way she is very sexy. A fellow chorine who danced with Audrey at the beginning of Audrey's career lamented that although she, the chorine, had "the biggest tits" on the stage, everyone's eyes were on Audrey.

The ravishing truth was that Holly wasn't merely anything. She might portray a call girl or a nun or a princess but all those roles partook of what a fellow actor called her "spiritual beauty." Right there in front of the camera Audrey's role was happening but something else was happening, too, something rare. Amid the celebration of the external that movies of necessity indulge, there was some internal spirit that was animating the call girl or the nun or the princess that not only would not equivocate but could not equivocate.

Spirit always steps in from another world. We don't know what that world is because all we have to go on are intimations. There was Audrey's childhood and the pall of abandonment that attended her, a sort of luminous shadow. There was her native élan. There was the feeling that she intuited more than ever could be put into language and so her facial expressions formed a higher language. There was her voice, which at times was so girlish it might have floated away.

There was the stark suffering of someone who has miscarried a number of times, who literally has lost life and been transfigured by grief. There was an edge that came from being treated roughly by human-unkind. There was the awareness that emotion can't stop tanks and bullets, an awareness likely to breed a degree of both despair and hardheaded honesty. There was her physical presence, how at any moment she was in touch with the gestures of dance: each movement could be precious. And there was something indomitable, at once tender and powerful and blind. She famously played a blind woman in the terrifying *Wait Until Dark*. Her feel for the role of someone who refused to be powerless yet was achingly vulnerable was flawless.

Audrey kept the press at bay and lived most of the time in Switzerland far from the picture-snapping crowd. She didn't want to be in that emptiest and silliest of categories—a star. Like any serious person faced with the helter-skelter of modern circumstances, she wanted to find out who she was. Though it was the long way home, being in front of the camera helped her.

She would have been quick to say that the camera only went so far. Although there was nothing inherently wrong with standing in the rain and kissing George Peppard, the box-office wisdom of happy endings was a species of tyranny. Anything that was decreed, even happiness, was bound to stifle true feeling. It was childish too. Audrey had two marriages and various love affairs. She knew how romance paled. Men could be oafish and selfish, or perhaps worse, bored. Her mother had loved her but was not good at showing it. Her father had left her. She had seen people taken away to be murdered and had grieved over her own stillborn child. She needed the warm proofs of love but, like anything human, love could become distracted. When it became distracted, it was lost.

She had a great deal. Women envied her. What she wanted—to be a mother and create a strong family—wasn't easy for someone with her career. And she liked falling in love. The movies were right: falling in love was one of life's high points, one she did on the screen and in her life with actors like Bill Holden and Albert Finney. No wonder women envied her.

The ends of those affairs were never happy. Sex was lovely but it curdled if there wasn't sustaining love. It curdled too because beyond a movie actress's trailer or hotel room or getaway villa there was the political world men had made. She had experienced that world firsthand and never forgot it.

Some people dismissed her when, as a goodwill ambassador for UNICEF, she was photographed holding an African baby: another white lady stooping to the pain of the dispossessed. That wasn't fair. No one made her go to Somalia or Ethiopia, places where something dire could happen at any moment. Since the world at large paid attention to her, here was something real to pay to attention to. She knew that suffering was not something the world wanted to ponder. That was why there were distractions like movies. The hell of children too weak to move, thin as spindles, nothing more than bones, doomed to die: it was ghastly. She witnessed the agony and kept coming back to remind people.

There was something beautiful, desperate, noble, and griev-ous about the work Audrey did for UNICEF. What kind of world tormented children? What kind of world felt there was any-thing more important than the welfare of children? She knew the answers but didn't despair. She was one of those people who though they have seen history's horrors remain hopeful: there must be more to being human than this. Her acting and her role of goodwill ambassador came from the same place: determina-tion to find the right human core.

Many actors get lost. What they pretend to be becomes who they are. They lose themselves in the mirrors they are always con-sulting. Audrey went the other way. By the time she died, she had found herself. The child became the adult who reached back to help the child. When she played Sister Luke in *The Nun's Story* it was out of a conviction that was wholly genuine. She gave herself up to acting as if to a religious vocation. There she could practice the notion of perfection. The notion, she admitted, was ridicu-lous, emphasizing her failings and insecurities. But no matter: every moment in every scene held out the possibility of reaching communion between herself and the person she was playing.

To tell other adults what you have lived through as a child is very difficult. A child's responses are at once profound and simple; they enact an instinctive philosophy. An adult's answers tend to be too dismissive or too hurt, too aware of the tangled enormity of experience. Audrey's response was unusual—to mingle joy with bemusement. Her magical, delightful smile was a latter-day Pierrot's, possessed of an uncanny blend of ungainliness and calm. She breathed the very lightness of being. In another century, she would have shown her sad, droll heart in pantomime. In the twentieth century, as a woman, she spoke.

WILLEM DE KOONING

A YOUNG MAN DECIDES TO STOW AWAY. He could scrape together the money and buy a ticket. Many people have done that so they could go to America, people much poorer than he. They sold whatever they had—a donkey, a table, a necklace. They borrowed. They stole. He is improvident, however, an instinctive romantic. He detests the very notion of saving. Or he feels that there is nothing to save. There is endless movement; light and air cannot be saved. He understands the word *ontology*. In his quiet way he revels in metaphysics but he doesn't care about definitions. He cares about paint. He makes signs and paints houses. Paint cares for the world. Paint is daily stuff.

Like everyone he has notions about America. Largely they stem from the movies. America is the land of fantasy, of Charlie Chaplin and Buster Keaton. He likes the humor, the drollery, the commerce between the possible and the impossible, the grimace of longing. Even from afar, he understands the loneliness of the place, all those little human molecules bouncing off one another as they pursue the chimera of happiness. Yet the absence of any overarching goal reassures him. Europe is the home of kings and their great, grinding purposes. Chaplin and Keaton have no purposes. The beauty they make is contingent on the mere fact of their being human, their walking down a street, looking in a window, eyeing a woman, tipping a battered hat, waving a cane. They have no apologies to make. Their vulnerability goes without saying; lacking as Americans do an aristocracy, their pretensions have no pretense. Despite the many stories he has read as a child about Indians and buffalo hunters and pioneers, the bravery of Americans does not impress him. They could not help themselves in that regard; the vastness of the continent demanded tenacity. It is their innocence that impresses him, their smiling blindness, their offhand candor. He sees all that on the screen while he sits in the stale dark and chuckles and roars. Chaplin fiddles with his tie; Keaton stretches his mouth until it is a sort of prairie. He, the viewer, can laugh until he cries; he understands what genius is.

Where he wants to go isn't the width and breadth of America, all those strangely named states he barely can remember; it's the former Dutch enclave of New York City. Among the advertisements and crowds, he can be who he wants to be. He can't define what that will be but he can say what he doesn't want to be. He doesn't want to be another bourgeois. He doesn't want to pretend to be more solid than he is. He doesn't want to surrender his life to history. There is the feeling in Rotterdam of trying to hold on to something that has died already. That is what makes his mother violent and his father distant. They are trying to live but they have no room to breathe. So they try harder and breathe less. They barely exist but they keep trying.

If he can see no further than the next New York City block, that is fine. The last thing he wants to do is wander and look. He does that inside of himself enough already. Amateur painters make a fetish of looking so intently at this flower and that tree. They don't understand how greedy the eyes are; how they subdue the hand, how they enforce imitation. *See:* often the word is a command more than a question. It insinuates authority: see what I see, see what society sees, see what you are told to see. He prefers the question.

Anticipating the modest amount of space infested by gargantuan buildings that distinguishes New York City pleases him. For him it is best that the rest of the nation remain in novels and histories. Like too much turp in the paint, being elsewhere would thin out the feeling. When he sits in a movie theater in Rotterdam and sees the cowboys galloping across the plains, he senses what may be one of America's dilemmas—the distances are bound to mock any feeling. The hero is always looking into the distance beyond the woman who stands there pleading. When he tells his friends about his plans to emigrate, they laugh and ask, "Naar Texas?" "Texas, nee" he replies.

Like everyone in his nation, he has lived his life not far from the sea. Though he loves the sea, when he thinks of a painting he loves it is an interior or a portrait. When a painter renders the sea by itself, there is the difficulty of what is faceless and the difficulty of where to begin. To frame the sea is a joke. The horizon appalls. The depths are unthinkable, the surface ungraspable. Faced with this chthonic indifference the painter offers his puny industry.

There were ways of course to win the game. When Vermeer painted his *View of Delft* the sea—still as a blanket on a bed—capitulated, yet what was gained? Vermeer's homage was an act of exquisite revenge: enormity economized. There was no self-consciousness in that painting (Vermeer was far beyond such vanity) but the scale of the human—those figures in the foreground pointing at this or expostulating about that—was so modest as to be humorous. Perhaps that was Vermeer's wisdom. The Netherlands was a nation of bustling havens. A viewer might think those painted people could walk on the water behind them.

The ships on the sea are toys. The sailors on the ships are less than toys. A stowaway is less than a sailor yet a stowaway must emulate the sea's silence. When he tramps around Rotterdam in pursuit of nothing special, he practices that silence. It isn't hard. Though he is gregarious enough, he has cultivated silence. It is the margin of his dignity. And paint is inarticulate. No one expects a painter to say much.

He wants to imagine himself into the world but it is hard. He doesn't have much to go by—poverty, lovelessness, anger, the callous maxims of realism. Those days and nights can turn a boy who is becoming a man into one more human projectile. To land as any projectile must land is to be impaled by more of the same, to live in another tiny room and smell the cabbage being fried and the raised voices. He has heard more arguments than there are stars in the heavens. He has been in his share of them. He has shut his eyes and raised his own voice. He has shaken his fists. Yet even as he did so, he felt there must be more to being human than this.

Imagination is an imperative and a siren too. The ships in the harbor are not much to look at—floating beasts of burden—but they offer escape. First a person has to escape before anything can happen. He has prospects enough in his homeland. He can make furniture. He can draw. He can design. He can paint anything. None of that adds up to imagination, however. It adds up to one week paying another. It adds up to the beggared love of begetting a child on some young woman desperate with desire. Or she may not even be desperate. She may be calculating. He has heard plenty of those stories. He wants women all the time but he is wary. Women have their own imaginations. They can turn men into pawns. Imagination must not be naïve.

How many days has he stood by the sea and stared, as if waiting for an answer? How many days has he gone to Amsterdam to the Rijksmuseum and stared, as if the paintings could speak to him? They do, of course. That is what great paintings do. They tell him of the impossibility of perfection, the semblance of it and the goad of it, the wanting. They tell him of darkness—so many of the paintings are obscured by shadows and night and a background that dissolves into black vapor. He sketches, the way countless acolytes sketch. He does not feel compromised by those who came before him. The past doesn't frighten or belittle him. If he is experiencing the past as he stands there, then it isn't the past. One day when he tells this to his mother, she says he has too many ideas. He knows better, though. If the paintings stank of the past, they wouldn't be on the museum walls. They would be in oblivion where most of the past resided, the detritus of moments and hours and days. Painting and drawing offer a release from that. They are a practical heaven.

On the ship to America there is no time for drawing. At first he hides behind some cargo boxes and then when the ship is at sea he emerges. The sailors laugh, spit at the floor and tell him they will put him to work. This ship isn't a luxury cruise; an extra hand is welcome in the boiler room. None of the higher-ups has to be informed. "Nothing worse than a snitch," an old sailor observes to the nods of the other men. Whether he has paid for his berth or hasn't makes no difference to their pay. If he helps them, he makes their work easier. If he looks down out of awkwardness and shyness when they make jokes about him, that makes their jokes all the better. If he thanks them for whatever leftovers they bring him from the dining table, that is something out of the ordinary—someone thanking someone.

Late at night he is able to get above deck. He feels excited yet sad. What has his life been thus far? If he threw himself overboard, who would mourn him? And the thought of how the sea would devour him is frightening. Still, he lingers for those minutes when he knows the watchman is elsewhere. He tries to stand back and see himself the way someone else might see him, there at the ship's rail. Not much comes of it: the only thought that visits him is his wishing he were taller. Foolish but such is what he thinks. When he hears steps, he retreats. No one hails him. If he doesn't officially exist, he is not there.

And if a romantic knows that he is a romantic is he still a romantic?

He has brought nothing with him. Though long planned, his departure has been sudden. *Now* a friend of his tells him and that is that. On the ship one sailor gives him an old shirt; another gives him a change of underwear. He becomes a mascot to the men in the boiler room. They know this is only a passage. They will never see him again. He understands that too. *This is how life works*, he thinks. *I have nothing and that is good.* He wants to make things but he wants to hold on to nothing. Or he doesn't want the making to ever finish.

The boat docks; the stowaway slips off, averting his face to any faces that might chance to look at him. A few sailors hoot and try to call attention to him so he walks faster down the gang plank. He sets foot in the New World. He exhales. There is nothing to constrain him. That is ignorance but also truth. His shirt and underwear are in a paper bag.

He is right about New York. It is his proper home. The city is careless in ways Rotterdam never could be careless. Everyone seems to know where they are headed. Everyone is in a rush but everyone is heedless too, busy thinking the next thought, living the next moment, ahead of themselves, in pursuit. He can feel that. He doesn't have to think it; he can feel it on a street corner while he waits for a traffic light to change. If he stands still for too long, people assume something is wrong with him. No one says anything but they eye him. He must be a foreigner or a simpleton, a lost soul. The eyeing lasts only for a moment. Then they are off to wherever they are going.

New Yorkers need signs to tell them what to do and see and buy. He is good at making signs, also at making displays for store windows. He is an artisan, though that is not an American word. His bosses appreciate the quality of his work though some want him to work faster. "Cut corners" is one of the first phrases he learns. "We need to cut some corners, Bill." He feels not just the hopelessness of trying to adapt to a different rhythm of work but also the hopelessness of idioms. Still, he tries. *Will do. Roger. Got you.* The phrases spin through his head. People like it when he uses them. They smile. He smiles back. This charade is a little demeaning but only a little. He knows that enthusiasm is important. He can be enthusiastic. He can reassure. *Got you.*

His melancholy would sing to him but that old-world voice is hard to hear in the hubbub. That is, as they say, okay. He must be resolute. Yet what he feels inside himself is not so resolute. It is not doubt but longing, not only for a woman—women are attracted to him—but for a life's work. He believes his hands will lead him there. Sometimes when he is washing his hands, after work or when he rises, he pauses and examines them. They are not beautiful but they are perfectly strong. He trusts them. Who else to trust? They are part of the body's persevering sanity, millennia of adaptation. One reason he loves to paint is because he loves to grip the brush. That sensation gets overlooked but never by him. Before the painting there is this blessed gripping.

Because of the new language he is like a child again. His accent is amusing—his *th* tends to be a *d, that* is *dat*—but he is definitely not a child. He could allow himself the resentment of humiliation but refuses. To quarrel with good humor is foolish and the Americans he meets at work are good humored. Working people are working people the world over. They know what the hour hand is, what a cup of coffee is, and what a boss is. And he delights in their vocabulary. One day someone says, "Hot diggity dog." The phrase throws him into a paroxysm of confused delight. He doesn't understand it but he intuits the excitement. It is a ridiculous yet sensible superlative. A few days later he says the phrase. His workmates laugh. They get him.

When he buys a new suit to wear on Sunday outings, he feels as though he is being reborn. He goes to have dinner with a friend he has made at work and with the man's family, a wife and two children. They all sit around a table and eat meat and potatoes and talk about nothing special—other people, movie stars, athletic events. Again he realizes this is part of his passage but he is on dry land now. He is moving forward. He is one among many. At home he felt too close to zero. However overwhelming the American numbers may be, the fact of *one* remains staunch. When he returns to his tiny room, he pauses and admires himself in the cracked mirror on the back of a door. He runs his hands over the jacket. He looks trim. He looks sharp. He can allow himself to smile.

He doesn't worry. He has money. He meets a woman who is good for him. Whether he is good for her never enters his head. He isn't like that. He explains to her that life is like a teeter-totter: the two people are together on it but one is up and one is down. Both can't be up at the same time. She smiles at him and shakes her head. He is charming; it is a rare woman who does not want to be charmed. He knows that but is not conceited. He is too intent on whatever is in front of him to be conceited.

What is the new nation telling him? What art is possible here? Everything must be useful here—that is the justifying work of the nation—and he agrees, but only up to a point. After he has taken the time to commend the cars and record players and elevators, he recognizes how these inventions are not all there is for him here. He must go past that point. Such going can make a person doubt himself. He doesn't come from the privileged classes. No one has handed him fine art on a plate and welcomed him to partake. He studied at an academy back home but that was more like the nineteenth century, the assured century, the century before the frame was shattered. In America, to broach the subject of art to any casual acquaintance is to invite a large pause in the conversation.

Gradually he does meet people who want to talk about art and who practice it. They often are displaced people too. "Washed up here," one of them puts it, as if he and others were flotsam and jetsam, what the sailors threw overboard on the ship from Rotterdam. He wants to laugh at that but recognizes the truth. To imagine that other people, the people milling around him on any midtown Manhattan street corner, would be interested in what displaced people do is hard to believe. That, however, is no reason not to start painting and talking with others who paint. He needs to do that. He must do that. The desire infuses and animates him.

These painters believe in modern times but not as something that can be made, advertised and sold. They believe in modern times as a metaphysical enterprise, a challenge. New times demand new ways of seeing and acting. The challenges, however, are daunting. How does one invent a tradition? Tradition is something that is handed down and agreed upon. It isn't individual. And where does one find the authority to move ahead? To be obsessed is fine in its way. He can bear being poor. He can bear going hungry. That is how he grew up. He has fled Europe but he never would flee from himself. And yet there must be more than obsession. Obsession can limit as much as enrich. Obsession can be cranky and tiresome.

The talk among the displaced painters is vivid and affirming. They face the same difficulties, revere the same contemporaries, even if sometimes it feels everything is contained in the protean name *Picasso*. Over and over they come to Picasso's door and stand amazed. They also go to the museum on Fifth Avenue and consider the tradition. Other people wander by the paintings talking of where they will eat lunch or shop but the painters stand for long minutes and observe an Ingres or Chardin. They are not interested in likenesses. They are extracting essences, critiquing forms and geometries, lines and proportions and edges and centers, compositions and brush strokes, shadows and volumes and foregrounds and backgrounds and space. And that is only a fraction of what they see.

What goes into the making is boundless. In a way, that is reassuring. The painters are like swimmers launched upon a vast lake. Reaching the other shore may be a delusion but that is all right. They belong there with the paintings in the museums. However obscurely, they feel that someday their own paintings may hang there. It is absurd—just look at their clothes and listen to their speech—but it is not absurd. America is an unsettled place where anything can happen. Like Picasso this country must continually reinvent itself. When the painters walk outside of the museum and stand in the late afternoon light on the great steps leading down to the street, they breathe deeply. The exhaust being spewed from cars, buses, and buildings is good. There is more life here than they ever can get down on canvas. That too is reassuring.

His own painting is wan. It is easy to say that the grays and rusts are part of the shabby, hopeless era, the lines of identical-seeming men looking for work or waiting patiently for a bowl of soup, but it is his soul that is gray and rusty. He labors at each painting but destroys most of what he does. He has guiding notions in his head—the masters are alive for him—but the gap between his head and the canvas seems unbridgeable. It would be easy for him to not trust himself. That happens sometimes. He bulls ahead hoping that the hard work which he adores and to which he is inured will save him. It doesn't. In what's left he sees little more than painterly ashes.

Other painters who come by to look at his work don't feel that way. They realize something strong yet exquisite is present. They realize that there is more sensitivity than anyone might know what to do with. The painters talk with him but however invigorating the talk is, it remains talk. The essential thing is to figure out how to be modern in ways that are convincing and individual and profound. The painters don't say that exactly but they feel it. To put together all three of those qualities is daunting. No one could be Michelangelo anymore: such ambition would literally be out of place. There are no monumental pedestals of spirit to stand on. Permanence has given way to impermanence. At best, modern artists can be grandly assertive in the way Picasso is grandly assertive. That is not all Picasso is, but that is part of it—the willingness to engage every dimension of life through the medium of painting. When they see his *Guernica* they weep inside. The power and the broken glory of it are irrefutable. That is what they tell one another art should be—irrefutable. Yet the world where they live practices its refutations daily. All Willem de Kooning has to do is open the window of his studio and listen to the automobile horns. He doesn't despise the horns but their tidings are empty.

He whistles while he works. He is full of good cheer despite what the paintings look like. He is a harlequin, always wearing two or more colors. His inner weather is the mist and cold that comes off the North Sea. His inner weather is joy in the physical facts of existence. He would not change anything and has, accordingly, little interest in the leftism of his friends. Progress seems foolish to him. The issue is to appreciate what has happened already and what is here now. Looking ahead is a sop, what the purposeful will tells the anarchic soul. His whistling is habit but it is feeling too. He likes Stravinsky and jazz and folk tunes. He owns an impressive record player good for the parties he and his wife give occasionally. Everyone dances at these parties. Full of fun, he dances too.

It is not just painting he faces. It is the task of the painting, how it seeks to maintain its history, how it must be fresh yet not, as they say in America, born yesterday. History's shadow is a welcome one to him, though that makes him, to use the strange word of Americans, un-American. As an immigrant he is nervous about his long view. Other artists make pronouncements but he is inclined to speak in riddles, axioms, and parables. He is uncertain, humble, covertly ambitious, and prone to looking at life obliquely: don't think you know more than you do. Each day he is busy with his brushes defining the indefinable. No wonder he paints over endlessly, changes what is before him over and over and then discards most of what he creates. He wants the painting to come alive and be still at the same time. He wants to make his own miracles. Is that too much to ask?

He sits in restaurants and eats good meals and indifferent ones. He goes to cafeterias late at night and over a cup of strong coffee talks more. Sometimes he goes into a bar where other painters go and has a drink or two. People brag, people gossip, people complain. What he prefers above all is to walk the narrow downtown streets alone. If someone he knows recognizes him, they exchange greetings but he doesn't linger to talk. He is possessed by a quiet torment. He is one who fell out of the cradle long ago and for whom there is no crawling back in, no telling himself that he is someone else. He is doomed to return to the painting at hand.

He loathes his own melodrama. Walking the streets in the quiet, after the midnight hour, he whistles.

———

He succeeds. As in a slot machine the three matching images come up at the same time: critical acclaim, museums and patrons who want to buy his paintings, and the work itself. He becomes someone whose name is known to people who are strangers. He has worked hard all his life to hold on to himself. At times this has made him seem selfish and cold. Now he has lost his hold. Strangers come up and start talking. Women lie down for him. Acquaintances act as though they are ancient friends. Friends look suspiciously at him. He has been identified, yet the whole gist of his painting is to not be identified with any one particular, to keep moving, searching, pursuing and resisting identity. Identity means that you are more *was* than *is*. He must keep testing himself but he knows no one cares about struggles, especially as the art world begins to take on a carnival aspect. You are supposed to be perpetually excited about who you are. You are supposed to be a continual, edifying, *avant*-everything event. But you aren't that person.

That person is someone like the artist he calls Andy Asshole. Andy professes to be unexcited about himself which translates into ironic excitement, the excitement of anti-excitement. Andy adores identity. Andy's work mocks any notions of inwardness. Everyone is a product. His studio is called The Factory. Externals are just that—externals. There is nothing below or beneath or within. By accepting and glorifying the beast of commerce, Andy has tamed it. He has given the world a canny, bright, heaping portion of nothingness. The efforts of a painter trying to get strokes and forms to come to magical life might as well be going on millennia ago. The modernist Willem de Kooning might as well be a cave painter.

One thing replaces another in America even if the thing is a person.

He drinks for days on end. He wanders the streets of lower Manhattan and hangs out with derelicts. He looks like a derelict himself. He starts fights. He collapses on sidewalks. He knows he is playing out a grisly notion of the romantic artist. He knows the truth of his squalor, however, in ways few people know. How could they? They believe that achievements make a person secure and important. They don't understand that there are no achievements. There is only the restlessness of the work, of trying to get the impossible right. They aren't haunted. The purpose of the country he has made his homeland is to allow people to live lives that are not haunted. The oblivion of alcohol recommends itself all the more.

What saves him is the sea. It is, after all, the same vast sea that took him to America, the sea that awed, frightened, and consoled him. Now he can gaze at it to his heart's content. It wants nothing from him. The consolations of nature are part of what lie at the center of painting—the dynamic between resisting and accepting those consolations. Painting is so human, so fraught with indecision, so laden with time. The sea offers its eternal terms. The sea teaches submission. If he must be someone who answers to recognition, he must be able to bow his head before all that dwarfs recognition.

He bicycles. He goes for walks. He makes paintings. He has rid himself of the excitement machine. If people want to see him as serene or wise or masterful or a captive of his reputation, that is their business. He would like to say that he loves the world less but he is an honest man who would never say that. He still feels a definite enchantment in the morning's light, in the colors on his palette and outside his window. He still feels the power in moving his brush. He still marvels at his hands and the tactile wonder of paint. There did not have to be paint, he says in his aphoristic way to his assistants. Considering that he is a famous person, he seems to those assistants almost child-like.

"He's the painter," he overhears someone say one day in the local post office.

"Imagine that," another person says.

Richard Yates

For you there was no putting a positive spin on a hard life, a cardinal point in the Richard Yates fiction catechism, as instanced by the sentence with which you began *The Easter Parade*: "Neither of the Grimes sisters would have a happy life, and looking back it always seemed that the trouble began with their parents' divorce." You came from divorced parents and knew something about that "trouble." Still, you sought to make a go of life in the approved, after-the-good-war way—marriage, writing corporate copy in a NYC skyscraper, fatherhood, suburbia. It looked good on the outside but the words kept tugging at your sleeve, you being one of the self-selected tribe who clung to well-shaped air while tethered to childhood obsessions and a flair for the make-believe, who sent out invitations to parties at houses that did not exist.

The literary saints, Gustave Flaubert or Henry James or Vladimir Nabokov, who hovered above the keys, were at once hedonists and self-deniers, masters who indulged and reveled in language while martyring themselves to the rigors that went with pursuing the well-wrought sentence. Writing was a penance, though the original sin was hard to identify. The occupational hazards that went with such a pursuit were steep: caring for the page might as much wizen the heart as expand it. The heart lay at the center of your endeavor (*Young Hearts Crying* was one of your unembarrassed titles); you were attuned to that warning. The cost of being a writer was a cliché but a cliché, tedious as it was, could be true.

The moderate demands of daily life attacked you viciously. Bills had to be paid and appointments kept; social obligations accrued like interest; one damn, conforming step followed another. In your other life, out of sight and improbable, imagination beckoned, scintillated, and goaded. Imagination also stalled, perplexed, and vanished, impossible to pin down or explain. You tried to find refuge in the huddle of time, in schedules, projects, and some degree of self-knowledge, though too much would spoil the endeavor. You knew that the writer of fictions, in particular, must operate in the dark, or, at least, a deep twilight. There were spirits, gods, and many imps out there, even if you did not believe in such ancient beings. No one knew how to placate them. They ate men like so much worthless cake. Success and failure were both warnings. Not long after Ross Lockridge Jr.'s *Raintree County* was hailed in 1948 as "a cosmically brooding book full of significance and beauty," the author, who had spent six years on his novel and received a pile of money from Hollywood, committed suicide. Two lives could be one too many.

Less than a decade earlier, you entered the lists (a phrase that at that time would not have appalled you), a youth possessed of a life, possessed of other lives, congruent and incongruent, possessed of language, possessed of an obscure spark that would not go away and that led you forward into feeling that, yes, among the many opportunities and vocations that lay before you, you were a writer. As a youth, you might have wondered what that would mean but already, even in prep school, among the woolly and the narrow, you had glimmers. Firstly, being a writer meant having a stance before the world's challenges—cigarette dangling, head tilted, eyes hooded but piercing: the body armor of a literary adolescence. If your chums laughed at the scintilla of self-parody, you could lance their fooleries on paper.

At a much deeper reach, you could delve into what got passed over, especially the settling of scores, particularly those that couldn't be settled, parents and family and all the mornings of waking up and wondering, *How did this enormous sadness come to be?* A retiring and gawky child, you had an early sense of life's gray limitations. The hand of implacable intention lay very firmly on your slender shoulders. You were going to write.

There was no shortage of heroes to incite you, the two main ones, Ernest Hemingway and F. Scott Fitzgerald, representing a dizzying spectrum of achievement and misadventure. At night you lay in your bed in your dorm room and wondered what of them might be there in you. The sentences already inveigled and almost taunted you with their semblances of perfection, Hemingway's so forthright and physical, a sort of geology of feeling, hewn yet obdurate, and Fitzgerald's more capacious and sinuous, but no less sturdy. Those sentences existed in books but were visions of grace. Hem and Fitz—they were close enough to you to have nicknames—had wrested something from the primal hoard of what could be said and how it could be said. And though you, the young man sitting in a wooden chair on a forlorn Saturday afternoon, couldn't quite articulate what was moving you, you felt it. Writing was a form of being possessed. Writing was a calling, a vocation. A writer was born and started learning.

Behind the sentences were the lives. You'd read about those in the pages of glossy magazines, particularly about Hemingway, whose life seemed a series of photographed poses proclaiming his unappeasable appetite. His manhood never took a minute off; his every spoken word was a challenge. He made you nervous but envious. Fitzgerald, who already had died, seemed a spirit from another era and that made you uneasy. So much occurred so quickly to the young man from the Midwest and yet it all took too long and gave off a whiff of agony. How could such a talent be gone already? Shouldn't there be some magic in the words to ward off the Fates? Or did writers invite the Fates? Was that what Hemingway was doing? "Here I am. Come and get me." The writing wasn't just about the writing. You turned another pictorial page of *Life*.

You're young, you're young, you're young, everyone sang to you, but in 1944 death was singing, too, and death was indifferent to everyone's charms and plans. Maybe that was the first lesson that a young writer needed to learn beyond the pages in which Jay Gatsby and Myrtle Wilson and Catherine Barkley all died. Handily, there was a world war to teach it. The class of 1944 was going directly from the dusty enthusiasm of teachers and chafing banter of classmates into some uncharted hell. One student who enlisted early had died already. It did not take long. No matter how much everyone scoffed and joked, there was that unreal feeling: *This can happen to you.*

As the boys sat in the school chapel and listened to the minister extol the dead young soldier, no one looked around. You might enter a war as a boy but you would come out—alive or dead—as a man. Everyone rose slowly. Everyone sang a hymn. Everyone avoided everyone else's gaze. Everyone shuffled out. You knew your duty: to start putting down sentences, some for the school newspaper and some for a story about a young man's last days. The words in the chapel were well meant but inadequate. You lit a cigarette and started to clatter on the typewriter. You entered an alert trance already familiar to you. You wished, though, you had a girl to communicate your death-wary soul to.

Your cigarettes and poses could not make up for the absence of a girl. One benefit of joining the army was that you were more likely to get laid. Supposedly, everyone in the army got laid but that wasn't much consolation. The facts were bound to be squalid and furtive. You'd rather take your peacetime chances with the opposite sex and hope some ribbon of romance might attend the proceedings, but if you were going to be a man—and you were—there was no choice. The war called and you came. The classroom debates about the lessons of history, the bull sessions late at night about who you were and who you weren't evaporated in the clarion light of that call. You knew, though, that you weren't going to give up the typewriter. Beneath the servitude to circumstance, there was the freedom of teasing out the words, erasing, crossing out, and purely brooding. The world would do what it did—and, as a member of the class of '44, you could hear the grinding wheels very distinctly—but you had the bounded infinitude of the dictionary.

In Europe, in the army you joined upon graduation from Avon Old Farms, you could die any minute. Guys stood in one place and were killed. Guys moved away from that place to take a crap or obey an order that later turned out to be misconstrued and weren't killed. Or they were. You were a joke of sorts as a soldier, clumsy and prone to daydreaming. You weren't killed, though no one said there was justice in any of this. Others, smart and agile, were blown to smithereens. You saw buildings collapse and the ground explode. A man's voice—Jack from St. Louis—that was there one day was not there the next. What could you ask the air? Where was that voice? You turned a page of *Stars and Stripes* (there still were written words) then paused to marvel at your hand. You didn't have to stifle the cry inside of you because you sensed it couldn't come out anyway.

And then? Every storyteller was acquainted with those impatient words. Events called the shots but naming a battle or a date didn't tell the story of each droplet of fear. Private Yates returned to the land of his birth, but inside of him there was no novel about the war. You weren't like that. A creature of accretion and attrition, you weren't someone who would be ignited by one experience, however enormous, however devastating. Watching your mother blither and dither as she shuffled her pathetic pack of social pretensions yet—to give her credit—hold on to some important scrap of herself as an artist, watching your father not do much of anything beyond work and appear at regular intervals, a decent but distant man, made you suited to writing a certain sort of fiction, one where people exercise much effort to go nowhere.

It was not an inspiring vision. There was neither Robert Jordan's heroism nor Gatsby's more-than-a-symbol mansion but there was the content—the feel of how lives unraveled—and the form—the challenge of learning the craft. You began where many began, writing short stories, trying to see how something partial can be a whole. There were the dead ends and misconceptions that were part of the process, but that, when you are living through the process, when you invest days, weeks, and months and wind up in some semi-well-written nowhere, can lead a person to rethink his choice of vocations.

Given the era's myths about booze and writers, a sign could have been placed over your often weary, baffled head that read, "This man needs a whisky." You never turned one down but what ate at you was more than embracing the role of hard-drinking writer. Bourbon was the beginning and end of everything, the healer and the miscreant, the all-purpose oblivion for someone more than half in love with oblivion. The daily sobriety that living required frightened you more than your own dark frights. Whatever blasted landscape those frights represented—your parents' divorce, war, your ungainly sensitivity—they were your frights. If the way could be harder and more self-defeating, that was your way. Life largely took place on such grim ground; every aspiration came with a hole in it. If you spoiled your life and others' that was a charge you, as an honest man, were willing to bear. The doom of drink made sense to you. You dwelled in the liquid fastness of suffering words; the bottle never complained.

You stumbled plenty: throwing up, ranting, arguing, hallucinating, passing out after a night's drinking. Once upon a time in the army, you strode—upright and quick—but hardly anyone did that in civilian life. Maybe you saw a few corporate types striding around the offices of Remington Rand, the corporation for which you ghost-wrote public relations pieces. You had nothing against purpose. You were full of it yourself but of a different sort. The industrial progress you trumpeted in article after article about the advent of the new this and better that—the UNIVAC computer!—meant nothing to you. You had elected to join a tribe of singletons who belonged to no department and reported to no boss. Who they were, until they emerged into the world of published daylight, was one more mystery. Who you were amounted to a larger mystery—a kid who went to war and came home and met a girl and started to write in earnest as an adult, as a man of the world. You lived in compartments—making a living here, writing there, marriage somewhere, drinking everywhere and nowhere. You never thought to ask what divides went through you. One miracle of writing fictions about others was how it could cancel out introspection.

You wrote about those others beautifully, as beautifully as anyone ever. That was a large statement but you held your shambling self to a very high bar. The disparities that yawned in front of each of your days were, in that clear, perennial light, ridiculous. So, when you wrote in your novel *Revolutionary Road* about the heroine April Wheeler spending a day doing housework she usually avoided, you wrote perfect sentences about endeavors that, given your total lack of domesticity, might as well have been otherworldly. April peered into an oven crusted with "scum." She discovered hordes of ants under a piece of loose linoleum. She picked up a waterlogged box that fell apart in her hands. You probably never had picked up a cloth to dust a tabletop. What was dust?

To any woman who knew you, beginning with the two who divorced you, the notion of you scrutinizing the arcane innards of a stove was somewhere between droll and absurd. You were the epitome of the double standard—one set of rules for the guys roistering in the living room and one for the women, or "girls," as you called them, cleaning up in the kitchen. Your written answer lay in the lucid sympathy you lavished upon April Wheeler and, in your other great novel *The Easter Parade*, upon Emily Grimes. In the face of the American happiness mania, you held up the flag that signaled the quiet and unquiet suffering women endured: you must be a good wife, you must be a good mother, you must smile for every moment, you must keep a spotless house, you must show a conversational interest in every dullard, you must do good works, you must consider every social nuance, you must always look your loveliest. You must, you must, you must. It could wear a heart out. April Wheeler killed herself. Emily Grimes led a life that never came into focus.

Those weren't endings many were keen on acknowledging and made you an Ancient Mariner figure: "Here comes Dick with his bottle of woe." You had to tell the truth and as a writer, writing sentence after carefully modulated sentence, you lived the truth. April and Emily and Pookie, Emily's remarkably embarrassing mother, were you as much as Emma Bovary was Flaubert. The distance you cultivated in your writing, your understanding how fraught human communication was, how people habitually talked past one another, how the agendas that drove their days lay always beneath the words, how human suffering was not a stain that could be bleached out, these were badges you wore with honor. Words on the page could, in their roundabout way, heal what seemed to you to be the inherent failures of our living with one another. You had a duty—an army word—to testify.

Cohabitating with such a brooding, yearning, damaged man was a bad idea but an enticing, alluring, lovely idea, too. You were alive in ways that surprised—a jack who kept popping out of the box, bent on entertaining the woman before him. You could sing show tunes all night, the more effervescent the Cole Porter-like rhyme the better. You could invent stories on the spot, where the feasible and infeasible could not be told apart. You could charm in that way men were supposed to charm, a composite of strength and boyishness, savvy and stricken innocence. You could charm because you felt that whatever beauty there was in the world was because of women. It was a compliment you discharged again and again.

A woman who lived with the empty bottles, black moods, and tetchy silences was bound to stop hearing those compliments. Your romanticism was foolish, immature, and selfish. When a wife—Sheila who bore with you for eleven years or Martha for nine years—would tell you as much, you were wounded. It wasn't fair! You meant well. Alas, your talent for being disabused, for elucidating to anyone who cared to read you how one blind moment connected with another in something people grandly called "life," existed in proportion to your unwillingness to locate yourself as an agent in those moments. The fatalism that sat on your head was a very unsteady crown.

Surely, life was not as dark as April Wheeler's death by a self-administered abortion. Surely, April's last feeling about life was wrong, "that if you wanted to do something absolutely honest, something true, it always turned out to be a thing that had to be done alone." Surely, life was not as bleak as Emily's "tired" admission at the end of *The Easter Parade* that "I've never understood anything in my whole life." Surely, you exaggerated. People moved to the suburbs and made satisfying lives replete with softball games, barbecues, and lawn mowing. Women lived in New York City by themselves and, unlike Emily Grimes, did not dissolve into bafflement. You acknowledged as much when you wrote about the housing development where Frank and

April Wheeler lived: "The Revolutionary Hill Estates had not been designed to accommodate a tragedy."

But what if you had the feeling, beginning with the agonies of a childhood spent moving with your devoutly impractical mother from one bohemian mirage to another, that life was largely a catastrophe, that *inevitably* every emotional exchange will be entangled in the fine print of misunderstanding? This feeling drove you not to a quick, definitive suicide but a slow, obscure one. Stubborn, unhappily enthralled, almost a hero, you remained engaged, however raggedly, with the pageant, with the parade. And making the sentences soothed something in you, even as it aggravated you, an attention that must be paid but that came at a price. A writer, as you and Flaubert and Fitzgerald and Dostoevsky saw it, was someone who paid the price—not just in labor but in summoning the spirits of contrariety that informed every human mischance. As someone who invited trouble—and what was a novel but the convolutions of trouble?—a writer was neither a scold nor a fashion-monger but a life-and-death conscience. To write about April Wheeler aborting herself was to take on that burden without flinching and without complaint. When you read once about how the British painter Turner lashed himself to a ship's mast to experience a storm at sea, you understood. Love wavered. Fame wavered. The hand that gripped the glass of Bourbon wavered but you believed a real artist never wavered.

The world thanked you variously for your hopeless commitment. In some corner of your head you expected front-page praise, dancing girls, and piles of dough. Men's heads were like that. You weren't cleaning a house, where today's mess becomes tomorrow's mess. The aggravations of the diurnal were a dream to someone busy making something meant to last *forever* in a society that had no clue about that forbidding word. You were making Something More Important, damn it. Falling down drunk, swearing, haranguing the well-intentioned, getting offended, taking an immediate dislike to this or that inoffensive person, sniffing out cabals where there were none, hectoring, making inappropriate passes, pleading, passing out, winding up in psych wards, these were exclamation marks to be inserted after the assertion of the importance of the endeavor. Life would never get it so you would show life.

Or you could not help yourself. Inside the wordy competence—the wrangling about commas and connotations—dwelled a great helplessness that attracted succoring women. There was a vulnerability that, amid all the posturing, could barely lisp its own name. There was a voice that came from this man who had gone to prep school (though not to college), had served in the army, had earned a living of sorts writing corporate copy, and dressed according to the buttoned-down proprieties of the era that was quiet and sensitive and harrowed by exigency, the voice of April Wheeler saying "Have a good day" and "So long" to her husband as he leaves for work on the morning of the day whose outcome will be her death by her own hand. There existed in that voice an unsettling mix of authority and wonder, knowing but also unknowing—a bow to the ultimate mysteries. Most of all, there was something recusant in the voice, something that refused the blandishments of getting-along accommodation, realizing, as April did at the end of her life, that unless you were careful, "the next thing you knew all honesty, all truth was as far away and glimmering, as hopelessly unattainable as the world of the golden people." Whoever, in April's mind, those "golden people" were, they stood for a wanting that was all too human.

You had more or less memorized *The Great Gatsby* for good reasons.

Though you worked for a time writing speeches for Robert Kennedy, you never were out to remake the world. You were out to present it through words, full as you were of gloomy love, to anyone near and far who had a hankering for knowing how people really lived and, as in the case of April Wheeler, that young wife cast up on a desperate corner of suburban Elysium, died. You believed in that hankering more than anything, not only as a moral imperative, which, as a drunk you were enamored of, but an aesthetic one, too. Every day was shot through with awe—"the smell of the earth" enticing the urban Frank Wheeler—which human beings could accept or, more likely, ignore.

Hollywood beckoned, big deals beckoned, options for movies that never got made beckoned, screenplays beckoned, even, academia, as represented most mightily by the Iowa Writers' Workshop, beckoned, a call you heeded for two years. As an autodidact, you didn't believe writing could be taught, though any page could be critiqued in 20/20 detail. Half-terrified and half-overbearing, you stood in front of the classroom and wandered through the gardens of fiction, confessing, in no discernible order, what you loved and what you hated. Those who listened to you understood, whether they agreed with you or not, that you were passionate. You were polite unless you were challenged and then became impolite.

The chatter about the community of writers was chatter; writing was a solitary activity that easily could shade—as you knew too well—into a lonely one. Putting a lot of people together who were most comfortable by themselves at a typewriter was a dubious idea. As an adverb-favoring writer might put it, *you smiled ruefully*, because, in truth, we weren't all in this together at all. There was no *we* and there was no *together*. This was America, where the atoms collided endlessly. American days were spume tossed up by a prodigious, pointless energy. How could anyone teach anyone about that? How could anyone in good faith offer intelligence about something so formless? Prefer real life over mannerism, you said to anyone who cared to listen while you reached for another beer.

There were, however, alimony and child support bills to pay, about which you were honorable even as you lived amid an ascetic wilderness: a bed, table, chair, and typewriter situated among empty fifths and cigarette stubs. Some part of you still believed in the dream of the Happy Family living in the Happy House, where time somehow existed outside of the pressures of time and money, habit and resentment. Your books, those long marches of writing where you felt on one blessed day you knew where you were and then on another wretched day that you didn't, kept undoing the dream. You were as tempted as anyone, however halting your pessimistic gait, to sign on the things-will-work-out-in-the-end line, but the hours the books demanded kept you honest. The work books required was work—to echo April Wheeler—done "alone;" the work that living with another person required could be very hard for such an "alone" person to do.

The continuing tap, tap, tap on the keys was audible but the true work was never heard or seen, residing as it did in obscure imagining and moving, slowly and far-from-surely, toward the realization of some hazy but powerful vision. Someone stood outside a bar; someone picked up a phone receiver and then put it down without making a call; someone put on a dress and looked in a mirror. Life had given you a family, friends, acquaintances, lovers, and you used them all for the fortuitous purposes of books. You had no right to. More than one of those people told you so. You may have protested that your aims were honorable or you may not have bothered. In your amber mind, the living were beside the point.

That sounds cruel but shouldn't. As a writer, you were doing people a favor, not that anyone would be accountably better for your excavating the human condition. It didn't work that way. The favor lay in your bothering and caring. Your role was not as a witness but as a seer. If no one looked deeply into the pool of being and no one created sentences that gave voice to that looking, then no one really understood anything. Most people were only repeating the blather they were born into, grew up with, and propagated as adults. The favor lay in your offering an alternative to the blather. You mimed the blather in your books, but, within that constant talk, you tried to find whatever homes that hearts had devised to survive in. You were a creator of homes.

And you were a patriot who had signed up under the Great American Novel Act. You never flagged in that aim—to give an imaginative shape to the destinies that rained down each democratic day, to create something compelling out of the unwary pieces. The visions that informed fiction were the society's lifeblood—whether it knew it or not. The first-rank value of fiction was not negotiable. Academia's explications and theories, along with the oscillations of reputation, were part of the explanatory baggage art had to live with. Fiction offered not facts or news or punditry about social forces but credible stories that were not only the stories of lives—Frank Wheeler's adultery and April Wheeler's death—but the stories people told themselves about their lives—Frank and April's story of themselves as a special couple or Emily

Grimes holding herself back from fully living. Fiction showed us how frightfully elastic the credible could be. Fiction showed us the stories inside each person.

At the end of your life, the friction born of that artistic aim had eroded whatever human credibility you once could summon. No one had told you to destroy yourself. No one had told you to sign up for Male Romantic Myth 101 or Platonic Ideal of the Novel 102. You had, however, sworn fealty to a lost cause or, more accurately, one that never existed in the first place, a remorseless honesty about the powers of self-deception. As Exhibit Number One of those powers, you couldn't help yourself. For you, being a fiction writer was like that: one made-up thing led to another. You followed the trail like some bloodhound from hell. You wrote marvelous sentences, though. You kept insisting that you hailed from heaven.

ANITA O'DAY

So TELL ME, SUGAR, what's a dame like you doing in a place like this?

A dame like me likes places like this, Jack. This—and Anita waves at the tables and chairs and bandstand—is home.

So you got some time, honey pie, to make some time?

Not with you, bud. Get lost.

Etcetera, etcetera, a wheedling volley of saccharine come-ons met by Anita's un-saccharine ripostes—every guy thinking if she's up on the stage showing herself off like that she must want what I've got to give her, she's asking for it—and on and on into the truly dark night of four in the morning when the clubs have closed and the music has vanished and whatever comforts may be found among the players and hangers-on are illegal or unwise. "Who are my friends now?" a dame might ask herself. She might even say it aloud to the bleak hotel room. This particular dame has a flair for the dramatic gesture. The skits she performs as part of her singing with bands like Gene Krupa's involve acting up and acting out. She likes that. Life is improvisation.

Anita O'Day was purely American in the sense of making it all up, including her surname which she claimed was pig Latin for money. It made sense that she would be interested in toying with syllables. Sheer playfulness was essential to her singing. As much as any poet, she engaged the sound-lives of words. The syllables dove, rose, stretched, thinned, juked and jumped, while Anita was deciding at each instant (while holding the whole sung line in abeyance) where to place the accent or emphasis. When she scatted, the syllables became ecstatic, seeming like nonsense but making emotional sense, the ride of felt rhythm. Across the water in France, the cafes were buzzing about something called "existentialism." Anita showed what the freedom of the moments could be.

The songs were there already, a geyser of tunes welling up in the first half of the twentieth century in America, a crafted, multifarious consideration of every conceivable angle of love, something similar to what happened with the Elizabethans and sonnets when the form and the feeling came together with a fine intensity. Anita was not alluding to Shakespeare each night, but the songs had Shakespearean range, sounding the blue depths of loss and the amusements—sometimes droll, sometimes celebratory, though more often rueful—of romantic misadventure and unabated longing. Every tune offered a perspective and so, along with whatever technical challenges presented themselves in three or so minutes—the are-you-sure-that's-the-right-key?—there was a chance to enter an original, articulate nub of feeling. Sometimes, the words gave people a purchase and perspective on their unruly hearts. Sometimes, the singer got through to them.

As a white woman, Anita was expected to be a housewife or a secretary or a teacher; by and large, that was what white women did. Negro women were meant to be maids or teachers in segregated schools. Prancing on a stage in the 1940s while trading choruses with Roy Eldridge, a genius Negro trumpeter, was not something women did. There was the race aspect and the female decorum aspect but there was the energetic of it, too. She was alive to this man and he was alive to her. It was all in fun, because America told itself everything was all in fun and that was supposed to make it okay, but their patter—"Blow, Roy, blow"—was hot stuff. This wasn't a church social much less a Sunday-morning hymn. They were riding a boogie, to quote a Krupa tune. Anyone who saw Anita up on a stage with Roy Eldridge had to sense that some public door was being opened that had never been opened before. There was the morass of bigotry and pontification and then there was this sheer joyfulness, as if to say, *Wouldn't you rather just dig life? We are.* When, behind the scenes, Roy complained about Anita showing him up, that placed their relationship in a long-standing, supra-racial situation—show-biz jealousy.

The jazz that Anita spent her life in was as much a verb as a noun. You took a song and you jazzed it, which meant you turned it inside out, an action at once elegant and visceral, brainy and instinctive. There was a world of technique in jazzing and Anita lapped it up, could never get enough of flatted fifths and bridges and stop-time. School hadn't done much of anything for her but that didn't mean she wasn't hungry to learn. School was not much more than a factory, a set of rote expectations, and that would not have been her scene. She hung around musicians and listened to their shop talk about the elusive intricacies and gradually became not one of the boys but a woman who could use her voice as an instrument as much as they could use a sax or set of drums.

Hanging out was something Chicago invited. It wasn't New York, which meant it wasn't the East, which meant it was more open to the range of American impulses. Chicago didn't know any better, unlike New York which, because it was New York, had to know better—that was New York's job. Like Anita, Chicago, as a hub for licit and illicit energies, could simply groove on the finger-popping brio of the vast nation. Conventions brought the crowds to the clubs. People worked day and night, so there were always after-hours when they needed to relax, to listen, to dance, and to indulge their urges and appetites.

The music Anita rose through the ranks with—the swing sound, the solid, gliding yet punchy 4/4—was anthem-like for her and millions of others. However it had evolved—inevitably from Negro sources but then appropriated by whites—it possessed a character that spoke to something indubitably American. Once upon a time, dancing had been either rural—turkey-in-the-straw barn dances—or formal—waltzing to the blaze of candelabras. Jazz gave the cities a chance to dance their own dances. The jitterbug that swept the nation was as alive as its evocative name. It could be toned down—and was in the hands of more sedate bands—but it could be swung frenetically, too—"Blow, Roy, blow." The swing bands seemed intrinsic to the American pageant as they traveled every byway to give performances while being broadcast and filmed and recorded. Bandleaders were giants. Talented instrumentalists became idols. Obstreperously vital, Anita O'Day was a natural for such a jumping scene.

At the tender age of fifteen, armed with her instincts and determination, Anita O'Day started singing while participating in dance endurance contests. She wore that out—to make the sort of pun Anita enjoyed—and set to learning music in Chicago's clubs, navigating her way through the tuneful, if emotionally slippery ("hey, baby doll") terrain and gradually making a living. What the guys had to teach her about music couldn't be duplicated. They *were* the music, happy to play and talk into the night. Their ardor matched hers.

She was not one to say, "Good enough." Although she could not have told you where she was headed, she knew she had to keep moving. She knew that the world that jazz presented to her was much more than getting up and singing a song. Canaries—the female singer who fronted a band—could be content with the melody, adding whatever flourishes they saw fit, but that was not Anita. It wasn't discontent that drove her so much as harmonic idealism: there was always more to find and to express in a song. If the nation was defined by its restlessness, the confused, gigantic vitality of so many people trying to find their ways in an unequivocally modern, machine-driven world, so Anita also was defined. Like the nation, she was proud of it.

That wasn't to say everyone was a hep cat. To listen and dance was one thing; to make the music was another. There were inner circles, with their rituals, their lingo and their trials, as in the famous cutting contests where musicians vied with one another in their inventiveness and technique. For a woman to be something more than a decoration took a boldness on that woman's part— not rashness but boldness. The music was everywhere, but how it fit into American life presented a puzzlement—commercial entertainment or abiding soul or a very uncertain hybrid. How a woman fit into the music was a further puzzlement: jazz musicians were men. There was nothing "lady-like" about the forces jazz unleashed. Jazz was loud, sensuous and all about letting go, while being a woman—officially at least—was about your un-sullied name.

Several ironies stared Anita in the face each morning. She may not have been exactly pretty, the way a canary was sup-posed to be pretty, but she was as alive as a body could be. That energy would seem to lead almost inevitably to love ad-ventures. After all, love was what most of the songs were about. The rapture sounded wonderful, but the songs were equally about the endless complications and unhappy finales, those I-thought-you-were-the-one confusions and sodden, autum-nal good-byes. And behind both the giddiness and disillusion, there lay the kicker of sex. Did every guy who wanted to go to bed with you, love you? Hardly, yet a woman looking for love—and Anita with her all-business, show-no-feeling moth-er and absent father was love-starved—could easily hope that making love might live up to its billing.

The couplings and uncouplings occurring in hotel rooms all around her demonstrated, if she needed to know, how love could not so much be managed as warily massaged. One way to deal was to be aloof or choose men who were aloof. Anita's first mar-riage was never consummated. What might have driven another woman mad with humiliation didn't seem to bother her. The sly mocking that often informed her singing wasn't a put-on. The songs were an opening to the world, sometimes brassy, but sometimes wistful. To sing many of the ballads was to engage something in public that was ordinarily private. Someone who played a weeks-long gig with her remarked that night after night she never sang a song quite the same way. Spun as they were from moment-by-moment sound and then vanishing, she possessed those songs and their range of sentiments for the time she sang them. As much as she lived anywhere, she lived in the songs.

Although she claimed that she cried sometimes—when the great sax player Zoot Sims died or when, in London, she happened upon the famous-through-a-song Barkley Square—she didn't cry often. Crying didn't help anything. Her mother had been stalwart in the face of raising a child more or less on her own and Anita, however she resented her mother, chose to be stalwart too. She was not raising a child but she was making a living exploring the by-ways of vulnerability; if a song had tears, she didn't choke up. She sang them.

The distance she cultivated in order to get by, her breezy, make-the-gig ways could not save her from emotions. For a woman making her own way, the trials ranged from routine to wretched. Some were built in to the biological and social fabric, like the double standards between men and women: guys did not get pregnant and have abortions; guys took it for granted they were in charge; guys thought dames were ditzy; guys could play around but dames couldn't. You could say something about it but the guys weren't listening.

There were double standards on top of those, which went with being in the jazz world—the main one being that straight people were upright, while by definition jazz people were not. The straight world was protected by police and rules and standards. The straight world was governed, and took its importance for granted. Every newspaper and classroom and political speech every day enforced that importance. The jazz world was ungoverned, unruly, and utterly made up. Its value, at best, was debatable. For many, it was worthless, another variety of race music to be denounced from pulpits or dismissed by classicists. A woman who stood out in front of a jazz band was a peculiar eminence—part female assertion, part one-of-the-band, part emotion conveyer, part song stylist and show-biz pro. No contract that Anita O'Day ever signed said, "Welcome to the contradictions" but there they were.

The straight world was ruled by grudges and Anita encountered them firsthand. One of the amazing conceits of the straight world was that it had the right to dictate what constituted proper consciousness. When you thought about it—and not many people did—it was preposterous, as if the state of someone's body-mind equilibrium or lack thereof could be calibrated and judged. Being normal—whatever the hell that meant—was okay. Prejudice and codified greed were, for instance, okay, as was telling other people who were minding their own business how to behave. It wasn't enough, though, for the straight world to hold all the cards. Examples had to be made; people such as drug users had to be shown as criminals, as flouting the rules of consciousness. If they were allowed to simply be, everything might fall to lotus-land wrack and ruin. Despite the series of political and social hells that made up modern times, no one controlling the hard-working, decent, God-fearing side of the street was interested in taking a chance: better ambition of whatever sort than sitting around and doing what seemed like nothing, better the march of progress than the mud of inertia.

The rules were laughable because, since they were human, they were arbitrary. The nation banned alcohol—what a notion!— but marijuana was okay. Then alcohol was legal but marijuana was banned. Whoops! Anita had been smoking grass since she was a teenager for the reasons most people smoked grass—it was a pleasant feeling that took the edge off the uptight, bustling din of white America's business-as-usual. Unlike the nine-to-five crowd, jazz musicians were up all hours exploring the inner space of music while entertaining people while trying to keep body and soul together. As a heady enterprise, weed's now-giggly, now-contemplative promotion of awareness made it a natural partner. All the affectionate nicknames—muggles, Mary Jane, pot, reefer, tea, jay—showed a kind of family intimacy. As a plant, it was part of earth's household.

Supposedly, it was sure to lead to worse. Look at Anita O'Day. She smoked marijuana and eventually became a heroin addict for fifteen years. That didn't keep her, however, from performing. She did a lot of her best work during those years, even when, in her blunt if banal words, she was "high as a kite." She didn't say she did that superlative singing because she was high, but it evidently didn't hinder her. Since she was out on some musical frontier every night as she took a song apart and put it back together, it would have been challenging for anyone to judge her or her state of being.

Busted a number of times, Anita went to jail. In her fashion, she made herself a practical help—cutting hair and organizing an exercise class—in the unappealing circumstances. Her arrests were accompanied by headlines proclaiming her sins: COPS NAB DOPE FIEND SINGER. Detectives pursued her and shook her down. She was to polite society an evil lawbreaker, the Jezebel of jazz as the newspapers (and some promoters) biblically put it. One of the psychic pistons American society ran on was stigma: a woman like Anita was easy pickings. Every law abider sitting down with the evening *Tribune* or *Herald* could draw self-righteous encouragement from her ordeals. Whatever the fallen woman got, she deserved. As the commissioner of the Federal Bureau of Narcotics,

Harry J. Anslinger, forthrightly put it, jazz was "Satanic." Jezebel meets the devil.

Had anyone wanted to actually talk with Anita O'Day, she could have told them that the only thing she was a fiend for was musical nuance. She also could have told them about the hard times that went with getting her hands on an illegal substance. Those good people shaking their heads and pointing their fingers didn't understand what a very equivocal pleasure heroin was, how looking for your next fix was a ruinous way to live, rife with anxiety and desperation. For a time the dark glow of the drug overcame those feelings but always the edgy duty of copping returned. Heroin put a person on a treadmill, in its way providing as much responsibility as any gainful occupation, since being addicted was a full-time job. Navigating through the underworld of users and suppliers, finks and corpses (Anita almost overdosed) offered the excitement of scoring but threw a sick cloud over every day, especially for someone who professed she wanted nothing more than to sing and make people happy.

However raggedly, the drug did fill up the hours. Anita was not the contented-little-housewife type. Captivating any intelligent ear and making meatloaf did not form a balanced equation. As a woman, given her narrowed choices, she was particularly susceptible to a drastic alternative, but many players were her cohorts. Heroin was a cult, a mystique, another knowing buttress against the unknowing straights. Given the music's often ecstatic intensity, oblivion may have seemed preferable to the errands and tasks that spoke for humdrum purpose. People bouncing around from club to club had a gig to make but did not have a set routine. While days elongated and evaporated, only the road, which led everywhere and nowhere, remained.

For those on permanent tour, America was firstly a map. People disappeared and then showed up and then got lost and then might be found or not, but the enormity of the country was in a weird, staring-out-the-bus-window way, comforting. If the straight world was out to own you, according to one set of directives or another, constant movement created an illusion that you couldn't be pinned down. There was always another town and another tune and another bunch of players, an underground of practitioners and devotees—the hip. Beyond the famous fraternal organizations that welcomed a traveler to Whatever Town, USA, there was the fraternity of music-making. Unless you walked away from it, once you were in, you were in.

Anita never had children and neither of her two marriages turned out well. She could be tempestuous and she could be indifferent. She worked closely with hundreds of musicians but she was bound to be in her own world. She used the fancy word *artist* about herself more than once, but this was a very hard claim to prove in the midst of changing into her performing outfit in a tiny room that had no lock on the door and was filled with cases of beer. It was hard to prove when a club owner said he couldn't pay you or extend your one week into two. It was hard to prove when the air that filled your precious lungs was rife with smoke and booze, acrid sweat and too-sweet perfume. The word *artist* had a nice ring—higher and better and more soulfully intricate—but you couldn't do much with that word on the street. People would laugh at you.

Those songs about romance at the core of Anita's songbook were a sort of blessing on the typically unromantic ways of an efficiency-worshipping nation. There was still something called "falling in love," as in her smooth yet snappy rendition of "Let's

Fall in Love." There was still the glimmering pulse of life, the beckoning that led men and women forward into bliss and misery. For Anita O'Day the notion of romance was, in many ways, ridiculous. She had been raped once and deceived often. Romance was confetti that lust left in its wake. But love was more than that, as her singing avowed. There was magic that confounded all the reasons in the world. She seemed to be born with a feeling for that magic. Maybe, it had no place in the larger scheme of serious things and maybe the songs and singer were adornments. Moving as she did between beauty and various beasts, Anita understood that. When she snapped her fingers and beckoned to the band, a rhythm was being invoked that was unique to her, a sense of time at once swung and suspended that informed more musical moods than any one woman had a right to. In song after song, amid the sweet welter of notes and tempos, she scaled the contradictions and emerged with a whole. What she had to offer specifically as a woman—her voice, her feeling, her being—stood for what typically was overlooked as the world of men went about its business. "Look, bud," she might have said. "Listen."

ACKNOWLEDGMENTS

THANKS TO THE EDITORS of the following journals where pieces first appeared, in earlier versions and in some cases with different titles: "Hannah Arendt in New York," in *Solstice Literary Magazine*; "George F. Kennan Takes a Train Ride," in *St. Petersburg Review*; "Harrisong," in *Five Points*; "Legend: Miles Davis," in *Brilliant Corners*; "Questions That Do Not Go Away: Audrey Hepburn," in *The Hopkins Review*; "Legend: Willem de Kooning," in *Grist*. "Legend: Willem de Kooning" was also included in *Best American Essays 2014*.

I read many books while working on the pieces that make up this book. The following were particularly helpful to me: *The Rebellious Life of Rosa Parks* by Jeanne Theoharis; *Hannah Arendt: For Love of the World* by Elizabeth Young-Bruehl; *Eichmann in Jerusalem* by Hannah Arendt; *Correspondence 1926–1969* by Hannah Arendt and Karl Jaspers; *Cold Warrior: James Jesus Angleton—The CIA's Master Spy Hunter* by Tom Mangold; *Legacy of Ashes: The History of the CIA* by Tim Weiner;

Acknowledgments

Disarmed and Dangerous: The Radical Lives and Times of Daniel and Philip Berrigan by Murray Polner and Jim O'Grady; *Widen the Prison Gates: Writing from Jails, April 1970–December 1972* by Philip Berrigan; *George F. Kennan: An American Life* by John Lewis Gaddis; *Memoirs 1925–1950* by George F. Kennan; *Tune In: The Beatles— All These Years* by Mark Lewisohn; *George Harrison: Living in the Material World* by Olivia Harrison and Mark Holborn; *Miles, the Autobiography* by Miles Davis with Quincy Troupe; *The Blue Moment: Miles Davis's* Kind of Blue *and the Remaking of Modern Music* by Richard Williams; *Audrey: The Life of Audrey Hepburn* by Charles Higham; *Fifth Avenue, 5 AM: Audrey Hepburn,* Breakfast at Tiffany's, *and the Dawn of the Modern Woman* by Sam Wasson; *de Kooning: An American Master* by Mark Stevens and Annalynn Swan; *The New York School* by Irving Sandler; *A Tragic Honesty: The Life and Work of Richard Yates* by Blake Bailey; *Revolutionary Road, The Easter Parade,* and *Eleven Kinds of Loneliness* by Richard Yates; and *High Times Hard Times* by Anita O'Day and George Eells.

OTHER BOOKS FROM TUPELO PRESS

Silver Road: Essays, Maps & Calligraphies (memoir), Kazim Ali

A Certain Roughness in Their Syntax (poems), Jorge Aulicino, translated by Judith Filc

Another English: Anglophone Poems from Around the World (anthology), edited by Catherine Barnett and Tiphanie Yanique

Personal Science (poems), Lillian-Yvonne Bertram

Almost Human (poems), Thomas Centolella

Land of Fire (poems), Mario Chard

New Cathay: Contemporary Chinese Poetry (anthology), edited by Ming Di

Calazazza's Delicious Dereliction (poems), Suzanne Dracius, translated by Nancy Naomi Carlson

Hallowed (poems), Patricia Fargnoli

Gossip and Metaphysics: Russian Modernist Poetry and Prose (anthology), edited by Katie Farris, Ilya Kaminsky, and Valzhyna Mort

Leprosarium (poems), Lise Goett

My Immaculate Assassin (novel), David Huddle

Darktown Follies (poems), Amaud Jamaul Johnson

Dancing in Odessa (poems), Ilya Kaminsky

A God in the House: Poets Talk About Faith (interviews), edited by Ilya Kaminsky and Katherine Towler

Third Voice (poems), Ruth Ellen Kocher

The Cowherd's Son (poems), Rajiv Mohabir

Marvels of the Invisible (poems), Jenny Molberg

Canto General: Song of the Americas (poems), Pablo Neruda, translated by Mariela Griffor and Jeffrey Levine

Ex-Voto (poems), Adélia Prado, translated by Ellen Doré Watson

The Life Beside This One (poems), Lawrence Raab

Intimate: An American Family Photo Album (hybrid memoir), Paisley Rekdal

The Voice of That Singing (poems), Juliet Rodeman

Good Bones (poems), Maggie Smith

Swallowing the Sea (essays), Lee Upton

Butch Geography (poems), Stacey Waite

feast gently (poems), G. C. Waldrep

See our complete list at www.tupelopress.org